Tom's Amazing

'What is this foolish business of girlfriends, boyfriends, two-timing, quarrelling, shouting? It is a ridiculous way to go on,' said Zenda.

'I agree,' said Tom. 'But I don't want anyone to hurt poor old Marion. She's my sister, after all.'

'Loyalty is good,' said Zenda. 'Very well – if this Cameron is two-timing, double-crossing, playing fast and loose . . . then we must do something about it.'

'What?' asked Tom.

'We will arrange a Revenge!'

Tom was somewhat alarmed. Zenda now sounded as though it was prepared to embark on a Mafia-style vendetta. 'What sort of Revenge?' he asked.

'I don't know yet,' said Zenda, 'but believe me – it won't be pleasant!'

'I believe you,' said Tom nervously.

Tom's Amazing Machine Takes A Trip

Gordon Snell

RED FOX

For Maeve, with all my love

A Red Fox Book
Published by Random Century Children's Books
20 Vauxhall Bridge Road, London SW1V 2SA

A division of the Random Century Group
London Melbourne Sydney Auckland
Johannesburg and agencies throughout the world

First published by Hutchinson Children's Books 1990
Red Fox edition 1991

Printed and bound in Great Britain by
Cox & Wyman Ltd, Reading, Berkshire

ISBN 0 09 974260 8

1

'What about a treasure hunt?'

'Or a sponsored marathon?'

'A pram race?'

'A vampire-costume contest?'

'A disco session?'

Tom and his cousin Emma were sitting in Tom's room, trying to think up schemes for making money. That morning at school, the head teacher, Mrs Forrester, had told them there was a chance of a school trip to Boulogne for the day. It was part of a national competition to see which school could come up with the best account of 'A Day in France'.

The school fund would pay part of the cost, and the pupils would raise the rest. Suggestions for fund-raising ideas were to be handed in tomorrow. Tom and Emma were trying to decide what to suggest. Suddenly a third voice broke in:

'These are foolish notions. You need something more intelligent.'

The voice came from Zenda, the lap-top computer which stood on the table at the end of Tom's bed. Anyone listening in would have thought it was Tom himself speaking, for Zenda imitated his voice perfectly. In fact, the machine could imitate any voice or sound it chose, and it was never slow to give out its opinions and views.

Zenda, Tom's amazing machine, was his constant

companion and friend. It had 'come to life' when some kind of life-spore from a distant planet out in space settled in to the machine and struck up a relationship with Tom. They had had many adventures together, first when Zenda was in a larger computer of Tom's which had been destroyed, and now in this lap-top model which would fit into Tom's satchel.

Only Tom and Emma knew that the machine had a life of its own, and they sometimes found it hard to keep the secret, because Zenda loved to show off and often nearly gave the game away.

So they were not at all surprised when Zenda butted in this time, saying a more intelligent scheme was needed. They both turned towards the computer.

'What do you suggest then?' asked Tom.

'A quiz!' said Zenda. 'I can think up the questions from my vast memory-store, then you can ask them, and the team that gets most right wins a prize.'

'I don't think much of that scheme,' said Emma. 'If all we do is give a prize away, we're going to lose money, not make it.'

'You humans have no logic,' said Zenda, giving a kind of electronic sigh. 'You would of course charge people to enter the competition – and the prize would be something not too expensive, like a computer game. You would make a lot of money towards your French trip.'

'I think Zenda is right,' said Tom. 'A quiz *would* be a good idea.'

'When have I ever had a bad idea?' the machine asked.

Tom could remember a few occasions when Zenda's enthusiastic ideas had caused a lot of confusion and chaos – but he was tactful enough not to mention them. Instead, he said: 'What kind of questions should we have?'

Zenda replied: 'I shall divide them into categories: say, sport, entertainment, music, geography, inter-stellar galactic cosmological phenomena . . .'

Tom and Emma laughed. 'What on earth is that?' Tom asked.

'It is nothing *on Earth!*' Zenda chuckled. 'It is all to do with space, where the really superior beings are – or were.'

'Beings like yourself, for example?' said Emma.

'Right in one!' said Zenda. 'A pity our planet blew itself to smithereens. Did I ever tell you how I floated round and round in space, looking for a new home . . . ?'

'Yes, you did,' said Tom hastily. Zenda was fond of telling the story of its amazing journey; the only dubious thing about the tale was that it had different variations each time it was told. So although Tom thought the basic facts must be true, he realized Zenda couldn't resist using its imagination to add extra colour and make them even more dramatic.

Emma said: 'Your idea is splendid, Zenda. I'll give it a fanfare!'

Emma cupped her hands to her lips and imitated a trumpet. She actually played the instrument very well, and even led a trio which performed at school concerts and played at dances too.

'Hey, there's another idea!' said Tom. 'We could organize a disco, and your group could play.'

3

'Terrific!' said Emma.

'Yes, not at all a bad notion,' said Zenda, in a rather patronizing tone. 'But meanwhile, we must get on with the quiz questions.'

'Okay,' said Tom. 'Fire away, Zenda. When we've decided on the list for each group, we'll print it out, then go on to the next. What shall we start with?'

'Sport,' said Emma.

'Very well, here goes,' said Zenda. 'I'll delve in the memory store and flash the questions on to the screen. Number one.'

Tom read out the words that came on to the screen: *Which Football Team Won The World Cup In 1966?*

'That's easy,' said Emma, who was a football fanatic, and one of the leading players in the school team ever since they had won the campaign to let girls play on it.

'Well?' came Zenda's voice from the machine.

'England, of course,' said Emma. 'Everyone knows that.'

'All right, then, number two!' said Zenda, sounding a little huffy. Tom and Emma looked at the screen, and gasped. Tom said: 'Oh, come off it, Zenda!'

On to the screen had come the words: *Who Played Left Back For The Real Madrid Under-Twenty-One Team When They Played Barcelona In 1979?*

Zenda said triumphantly: 'Well, you said you didn't want the questions too easy!'

'Yes, but that one is ridiculous,' said Emma.

'Even most computers wouldn't know things like that,' said Tom.

'You're dead right,' said Zenda with a squeaky

chuckle. 'I don't even know it myself. I just made up the question for fun.'

Emma laughed, but Tom said: 'It's going to be a terrific quiz if it's full of silly questions no one knows the answer to.'

'Yes,' said Emma, 'we'd have to give everyone their money back.'

'Ah well,' said Tom, giving Emma a wink. 'We'll just have to make up the questions ourselves.'

'No, wait!' came the voice from the machine. Tom smiled. He had judged, rightly, that Zenda couldn't bear to be left out.

'That was just my little joke,' the machine said. 'I cannot help it if you humans do not share my highly developed sense of humour. Of course I shall assist you in finding questions – and checking your answers are right.'

'Yes, we don't want any arguments,' said Tom.

'But supposing there *is* an argument about an answer?' Emma wondered. 'We can't tell everyone to wait while we run back here and ask Zenda to sort it out.'

'We'll take Zenda with us!'

'Good thinking, Tom,' said the machine. 'I shall make a superb quizmaster.'

'I'm sure you would, but we must keep you under cover. I'll have you in my satchel under the table, and if there is any problem, I can secretly look in and see what you suggest on your screen.'

'Who's going to be quizmaster then?' Zenda sounded a bit put out not to be given the starring role.

'One of the teachers, I suppose.'

'Miss Macdonald?' Emma suggested.

'She's very nice, but she's not great at controlling things.'

'Mr Roland?'

'No, he'd only start showing off.'

'Well, what about Mr Bainbridge then? He's dead keen to help if he thinks something is educational. Look how he helped us with the play, making chariots and all that.'

'Yes, Mr Bainbridge is a good idea. He'll keep it on the right lines. We'd better make sure we have a good few science questions – otherwise he'll say it's all too trivial.'

'No problem,' came Zenda's voice. 'My scientific knowledge is truly remarkable. Who invented the steam engine? How does the hovercraft work? What is the genetic code? Where did the first manned flight take place . . . ?'

'Hold on a minute!' said Tom. '*We* want to think up some questions too.'

'All right, but don't be too long about it. We machines are so much quicker at this sort of thing.'

Tom decided to ignore this jibe. 'We'll take it in turns to make up questions,' he said. 'Let me see . . . Yes, here's one. What does water consist of?'

'Two parts hydrogen and one part oxygen to each molecule,' said Zenda. 'That's one point to me.'

'It's not a competition,' said Tom. 'Though I'm sure you'd win if it was.' Flattering the machine was sometimes the best way to get its co-operation.

'Thank you for conceding victory,' said Zenda. 'Now, let's get quizzing, shall we?'

By the time Tom's mother called him for tea, they

had thought up nearly fifty questions. They left Zenda to print them out, and Emma said she'd better be getting home for her own tea. They would see Mr Bainbridge first thing in the morning with the list of questions, and hand in their other fund-raising suggestions, too.

At tea, Tom tried out a few of the questions on his mother and father, and his sister Marion. His father knew most of the sporting ones, his mother was good on geography, and Marion did well with the entertainment questions. She said they ought to have some questions about dress and fashions. She told Tom she would think some up for him.

'Thanks,' said Tom. 'But don't make them too hard.' Marion worked in an up-market dress shop, and was even designing clothes herself. She was always talking about trends and fashions – when she wasn't talking about her boyfriend Cameron.

Tom had an idea. 'Maybe Cameron could suggest some questions about motorbikes.'

'I'll ask him. He's calling for me later.'

'You will wear your helmet, won't you?' said their mother anxiously. She hated Marion riding on the back of Cameron's bike. So did their father, though Cameron kept reassuring them that he only ever went at speeds well below the limit. Tom doubted this. Whenever he watched them roar off from the house, they looked as if they were practically doing a ton by the time they reached the end of the road.

'Of course I'll wear my helmet, Mum,' said Marion.

'You should try designing those sometime,' said Mr Martin. 'That one you've got makes you look like an alien who's splashed down in a paint factory!'

'I've told you, Dad, it's very trendy.' The helmet had weird splodges and twisty patterns on it in the brightest day-glo colours, and a big fancy *M* in gold. Cameron had given it to her for her birthday, and Marion wouldn't hear a word against it.

'They certainly wouldn't let you into our works wearing that headgear,' said Mr Martin. 'In fact, these days they even make it hard to get in for people who actually work there!'

'How do you mean, Bill?' asked Tom's mother.

'Oh, there's high security. Particularly coming out. There's electronic screening gear, and all kinds of stuff.'

'Why? You only make cars, not atomic weapons.'

'You wouldn't think so if you saw the way they're going on now. You can't blame them, I suppose. There's been valuable components disappearing from the factory, apparently. They can't figure out who's doing it, or how.'

Tom listened eagerly. This was the kind of mystery which Zenda might be able to solve. But he could hardly suggest to his father that he take the computer in as a detective.

'I said, "Do you want some more pie, Tom?"' His mother's voice broke into his daydream.

'Thanks, Mum.' He realized he could only get Zenda to help if he did it in a roundabout way. After all, his father didn't even know Zenda had a mind of its own, let alone that it could talk. He decided to try gradually to get as much information as he could from his father about the thefts from the factory. If he fed this into Zenda, the machine might be able to suggest a line of enquiry, anyway. Meanwhile, he must get on with compiling some more questions for the quiz.

He and Emma met at school half an hour early, and went to see Mr Bainbridge, the science teacher.

'A quiz, eh?' he said. 'Good idea. Could be highly educational.' Tom and Emma glanced at each other. Their approach had been the right one.

Mr Bainbridge looked down the list of questions, grunting and nodding approvingly. Then he said: 'Excellent! I shall certainly back you with this idea – provided I think whoever runs the quiz can do the job properly. There are some people – no names, of course – that I wouldn't trust to run an egg-and-spoon race without causing a steward's inquiry.'

'Well, we were thinking, sir . . .' said Emma.

'. . . that you might consider running it yourself,' said Tom.

Mr Bainbridge beamed, and raised a hand to smooth the scanty hair on his forehead.

'Me? Well, that's extremely nice of you. And I may say, rather perceptive. I always fancied I could stand in for that television fellow who raps out all those questions.'

'Then you'll do it, sir?'

'Certainly.'

'A quiz?' said Joe Crabbe, in the playground later on. 'What a wet idea.'

9

'Wet as water!' sneered his henchman, Oily Watson, who always followed Joe slavishly.

'Well, I think it's terrific!' said Dicey Renton, and several of the others agreed.

'Anyway, Joe,' said Alice Hodgkins, 'I'm sure it's better than any idea *you* had.'

'Yes,' said Tom. 'Tell us what you suggested, Joe.'

Emma said: 'I bet he never suggested anything.'

'I did!' snapped Joe.

'What was it then?'

'A doughnut-eating race,' said Oily.

'You'd win that all right, Joe,' said Emma. 'You're as round as a doughnut already.' Everyone laughed.

'Shut up!' Joe snarled. 'I'll mash *you* into a doughnut if you're not careful!' Then he rounded on Oily. 'What do you want to go and tell them for?'

'But you said you were sure it would be the best suggestion. I thought . . .'

'Well, don't think – it might strain your brain.'

'Sorry, Joe.'

Dicey Renton said: 'Tell you what, Joe. We'll support your doughnut race, if you support the quiz. I reckon I could give you a run for your money in doughnut eating.'

Tom believed him. Dicey was usually munching something, and indeed at this moment he was taking a crumbly biscuit from his pocket and putting it into his mouth.

'All right, you're on,' said Joe. 'Bet I can win your stupid quiz with my eyes shut.'

The head teacher had asked everyone to gather in the

main hall after school, so that she could announce the fund-raising schemes that had been approved.

'First of all,' said Mrs Forrester, 'I'm pleased to say that there was an excellent response from you all. There have been many good ideas, and I have no doubt we shall be able to raise the necessary money for the trip to Boulogne.'

There was a lot of clapping, and excited chatter.

Then the head began to list the schemes that had been selected. The disco session was one of them, and there were ideas for raffles, fun runs, bingo, tombola, a face-painting competition, and a goal-kicking contest.

'And finally,' said Mrs Forrester, 'here's a scheme which will test your memory powers. It's a quiz, and it's been devised by Tom Martin and Emma Gratton. They've submitted some sample questions, and they cover all kinds of subjects, so I think that will be a lot of fun.'

There were murmurs of interest round the audience.

Mrs Forrester went on: 'They have also said there will be a really good prize.' The murmurs of interest grew louder.

Dicey Renton turned to Tom and asked eagerly: 'What's the prize?'

'Er . . . it's a secret,' said Tom. He suddenly realized they hadn't thought about that properly. How could he and Emma get a 'really good prize'? Zenda had suggested a computer game, but they'd have to think of something a bit more lavish than that. Then he had an idea: if they collected all the entrance money in advance, they could spend a good bit of that on the prize.

11

But his spirits fell when he and Emma went to see Mrs Forrester later on, to settle the details.

'Well, you two have certainly been busy with your ideas,' said the head. 'Your disco session should be popular, and I'm sure the quiz will be, too. It's good of you to donate a prize, because of course we couldn't let you use any of the money people pay to enter the contest; that all has to go to the Boulogne fund, otherwise it wouldn't be fair.'

'Yes, of course, we realize that,' said Tom glumly.

'Now, let's talk about the arrangements.' Mrs Forrester consulted a chart on her desk. 'I thought you could hold it after school on Tuesday afternoon, if that suits you. It gives everyone enough time to get their teams together. We thought teams of five would be about right, so that they can confer together about the answers. I gather Mr Bainbridge has agreed to act as quizmaster, so perhaps you could fix the rest of the rules with him.'

Mr Bainbridge had a lot of ideas, mainly to do with his own performance. He was behaving as if he was about to star in a television panel game.

'I shall preside standing at a lectern on the stage of the school hall, with the spotlights on, so that everyone can see. You two will sit at a table beside me, with the questions and answers, which you will hand to me. And you will also keep the score, which I will read out from time to time, to generate excitement.'

'Can we have buzzers for each team, sir?' Tom asked.

'Excellent notion,' said Mr Bainbridge. 'That will be something for my practical science classes to make.'

'Maybe we could have a gadget to give one sound when the answer's right, and another when it's wrong,' said Emma.

'Indeed!' said Mr Bainbridge. 'I'll organize that too. Oh, this will be the quiz of the century!'

Zenda was scornful of the buzzer idea. It said: 'I could make better noises than any which this Bainbridge person can devise!'

Tom said: 'Oh, we know that, Zenda, but Mr Bainbridge doesn't. He won't even know you're there.'

'Let's get on with thinking up more questions,' said Emma.

'There's one thing worrying me,' Tom said. 'The prize.'

'A computer game, as I told you before,' the machine said.

'I don't think that would be quite enough. We promised a really good prize – but how are we going to afford it?'

Tom and Emma sat frowning with concentrated thought. Zenda had one of its rare silences too. But then a series of high-pitched bleeps came from the machine.

'I think Zenda has an idea,' Tom said. He looked at the screen. Printed out on it were the words: FIND A SPONSOR!

'Well?' said the machine's voice. 'Aren't you going to congratulate me?'

'Yes, yes, you're brilliant,' Tom said hastily. 'But who can we find to sponsor us?'

'Would we have to wear names and a logo all over

our clothes, like footballers and athletes?' Emma asked.

'I somehow doubt if the school would let us,' said Tom.

'The name would be on the prize,' said Zenda.

'That's it!' said Tom. 'The name of a shop! We could get a shop to give a voucher for people to buy things there.'

'What about that new book and record store that's opened in the shopping centre near school?'

'Yes – Javed's uncle runs it. You know, the boy who's just started in our class.'

'Javed Patel?'

'That's him.'

Zenda said: 'A new shop needs publicity. This is ideal.'

'We'll get Javed to introduce us,' said Tom. 'Zenda, I think you've solved our problem.'

'Any time!' said the machine, pleased with itself.

At lunch break next day, Javed took them to meet his uncle Zia. The shop was crammed with shelves and racks of books and tapes and records.

Zia Patel was a big, beaming man, who shook hands with each of them, and then bent forward earnestly to hear what they had to say. As they explained the scheme, he kept nodding vigorously, and murmuring: 'A-one, A-one, A-one.' When they had finished he said: 'Yes indeed, a top-rate notion. I will certainly be glad to donate a prize voucher for the purchase of goods here.'

'Thanks a million, Mr Patel,' said Emma.

'But I think you may have a problem,' said Mr

14

Patel. 'Even perhaps a diplomatic incident, a potential cause of disputation.' Tom thought Javed's uncle seemed as fond of long words as Zenda.

He said: 'How do you mean, Mr Patel?'

'Well, you say there are five in each team.'

'That's right.'

'But will five individuals ever agree on what to buy with one voucher?'

'I hadn't thought of that.'

'Never mind, I also have a solution. I shall give you five vouchers instead of one.'

'That's terrific, Mr Patel,' said Emma.

'Wonderful!' said Tom.

'I look forward to seeing the winners here, in due course.' He beamed and again shook hands with Tom and Emma, then opened the door to show them out.

As they walked away, Tom and Emma thanked Javed for introducing them to his uncle.

'He's ever so generous, isn't he?' said Emma.

'Oh, he's great. My father says if he doesn't watch out, he'll find he's given away half his stock and have to close down.' Javed spoke warmly of his uncle, but Tom thought he looked a bit despondent.

'Is anything the matter, Javed?'

'No – nothing.'

'Come on. You can tell us.'

Javed stopped walking. 'Well, it's just that . . . if my uncle is giving the prizes for the quiz competition, I won't be able to go in for it. If my team won, everybody would say it was fixed.'

'Oh dear, I suppose you're right,' said Emma.

'I know!' Tom exclaimed. 'You can be on the

platform with Emma and me. You can be the scorer. We're going to have our work cut out organizing the questions for Mr Bainbridge anyway. It would be great to have someone else to keep score. We'll put you at a special table on the stage. How about that?'

Javed's beaming smile was almost as wide as his uncle's.

'That would be . . . A-one!' he said.

2

The quiz stirred up a lot of excitement in the school. Teams were formed, and every break time you could see huddles of five scattered around the playground, practising questions. They used old quiz books and Trivial Pursuit cards, certain that these were the sources Tom and Emma would be using. They didn't know they had another source: Zenda, the computer.

Question-making sessions with Zenda were fun – but they took a lot of time because the machine liked to show off by inventing long and complicated questions about subjects like particle physics, or comparative philology. Or else it would go to the other extreme, and start suggesting old idiotic riddles like:

'How do you know when an elephant's been in the fridge?'

'I don't know, Zenda. How?'

'Footprints in the butter.'

Finally all the questions were chosen and printed out. Then Tom and Emma got a big pile of library index cards from Miss Macdonald, cut up the print-outs and stuck one question and answer on each card. Mr Bainbridge had insisted on this. He said it was what all the professional quizmasters had.

'Between you and me,' Tom said to Emma one day, 'I think Mr Bainbridge is going a bit loopy.'

A series of bleeps came from Zenda. Tom knew the sounds. They meant the machine had come across a new word and was looking it up in its dictionary store. It was only a few moments before Zenda was displaying its findings, by saying:

'Loopy, eh? A-ha! You mean he has flipped his lid, gone round the bend, he's gaga, off his tree, doolally, not the full shilling, daft as a brush, fit for the funny farm . . . ?'

'Exactly!' Tom interrupted the flow.

'In what way does he demonstrate this curious state?'

'Well, he's obsessed with his quizmaster act. He wonders what he should wear, who he should talk like, what lighting he should have . . .'

'And he even wants me to play a fanfare on my trumpet before he comes on to the stage,' Emma said.

Zenda said: 'I do not think this is foolish behaviour. It is simply showmanship. There's nothing wrong with that!'

Tom and Emma looked at each other with some concern. They were afraid Zenda might try to rival Mr Bainbridge with some kind of theatrical caper. It was a risk they would just have to take.

After school on the day of the quiz, the hall was buzzing with chatter as the various teams gathered in groups. Some had taken folding chairs from the stacks at the sides of the hall and arranged them in tight circles so that they could confer easily. Other teams preferred to stand or squat down.

Tom and Emma were sitting to the right-hand side of the stage, at a table covered with a green baize cloth. The cloth hung down to the floor to conceal Zenda, which Tom had in his satchel on a stool underneath the table. The front of the machine was poking out enough for the small screen to be folded out, so that Tom could look down if Zenda wanted to communicate. Zenda had been given the strictest instructions not to talk aloud or make any sound.

In the middle of the stage was the lectern, ready for Mr Bainbridge, who was waiting backstage to make his entrance. And on the other side of the lectern was a table where Javed was sitting, looking neat and nervous. He had several ruled sheets in front of him, and lots of coloured pens and pencils in a jar. Behind him was a large board with three vertical slots on it, where square cards could be fitted.

Javed had made twenty-two of these cards, each with a big letter of the alphabet drawn on it. The teams had each been given a letter, so the twenty-two teams in the contest went from A through to V. Each team also had its own much larger card, like a placard, with its letter on. The idea was that after each round, Javed would put three letters into the slots on his scoreboard, to show which teams were leading.

'PSSSST! READY!'

Tom heard the hissing whisper from the curtains at the side of the stage. He nodded to Emma, who picked up her trumpet and blew a truly royal fanfare. The audience was hushed. Then, as the fanfare ended, out walked Mr Bainbridge. Tom stared. So did Emma and Javed – and so did the audience.

Mr Bainbridge was wearing a long black gown with wide flapping sleeves – and on his head was a wig. It was a judge's wig, the kind with long curled sides hanging down to the shoulders like the ears of a

19

huge spaniel. Tom thought he must have hired it from a theatre costume firm; or perhaps he even knew a judge who had lent it to him. In his hand he carried a black walking stick with a silver handle.

Mr Bainbridge strode to centre stage and threw out his arms in a big gesture. There were cheers, catcalls, whistles and boos from the audience, who were clearly astounded by the spectacle of their transformed science teacher.

Mr Bainbridge held his hands forward and made a patting gesture, calling for silence, but the row went on, mingled with a few shouts:

'Here comes the judge!'

'Give him thirty years!'

'Who's your hairdresser, ducky?'

Finally the noise subsided a little, and Mr Bainbridge could make himself be heard.

He cried: 'Thank you, thank you, for that warm reception! And tonight, as you know, is . . . The Quiz Of The Century! I am your genial host and quizmaster, and I shall preside over this feast of intellectual fun, with the aid of my trusty helpers, Tom Martin, Emma Gratton and Javed Patel. Give them a big hand!'

There were more cheers and catcalls, and the odd cry of 'Get off!' Tom, Emma and Javed all stood up and bowed, grinning and feeling a bit foolish.

Then Mr Bainbridge said: 'And now, it's on with the show! Can we have the first question, please?'

He held out his hand, and Tom reached across and gave him the first card from the pile.

Mr Bainbridge read it to himself, then announced:

'The first category is: Science.' There were some groans from the audience; Mr Bainbridge frowned, and continued: 'What is meant by a light year?'

From the hall there was the sound of several buzzers as the teams showed they knew the answer. They waved their placards in the air, and Mr Bainbridge pointed to the team holding up the T placard.

Don Matlock raised his hand. He was good at science, as well as being a top table-tennis player and the goalkeeper for the school football team. Someone in the audience called:

'Put it in the net, Don!'

Don Matlock smiled, then said: 'A light year is a measure of distance in astronomy. It is the distance light travels in the space of a year.'

Don's team-mates cheered and slapped him on the back, as Mr Bainbridge said loudly: 'Correct! Two points!' Tom pressed a pinger bell, which Mr Bainbridge had selected as the sound to be made when an answer was correct. Another gadget with a horn and a plunger on it, made the sound for a wrong answer. It was fairly disgusting, like a long-drawn-out deep burp. Mr Bainbridge seemed to think no quiz was complete without these additional sound effects.

The science questions continued, and at the end of the round Mr Bainbridge turned to Javed for the score. Javed handed him a slip of paper, and he read out the results. Don Matlock's T Team were well in the lead, with eight points. Then came Dicey Renton's D Team and Linda Morrison's J Team, with four points each.

There were cheers from Don's team, and grudging applause from the rest of the competitors. Javed put up the letters on his scoreboard. Tom handed Mr Bainbridge a new card.

The science teacher looked at it and said: 'The next category is: Sport.'

There was a buzz of excitement in the hall. Every team thought they could do well at this one.

Mr Bainbridge said: 'First question: What is a slalom?'

A buzzer went immediately, and the letter M was raised. Tom saw that it was being held up by Oily Watson, in Joe Crabbe's team. Oily was jumping up and down, but Joe was looking puzzled.

'M Team!' said Mr Bainbridge. 'What's the answer?'

Oily was about to speak, when Joe broke in: 'The Captain gives the answer!'

'Well, Crabbe, what *is* the answer?'

Joe turned to Oily, and said: 'Come on, come on!' Oily whispered in his ear.

Joe said loudly: 'A slalom is a Jewish greeting used on the sports field, sir.'

There was a burst of laughter, and some catcalls.

'Wrong!' said Mr Bainbridge. 'I believe you're mixing it up with *Shalom*.'

Tom pressed the plunger on the horn, which gave out the burping sound for an incorrect answer. There was more laughter. Then, to Tom's surprise, a series of further burps and gurgles sounded. Tom realized that Zenda had decided to help with the sound effects. He smiled sheepishly; he had to pretend that he'd made the noises himself.

22

Mr Bainbridge said: 'No need to over-do it, Tom.'

'Sorry, sir,' said Tom. He glared down at the glowing screen below the table. On it were the words: *Tee-hee!*

Down in the hall, he could see some disturbance in M Team. Joe Crabbe had hold of Oily's right ear and was twisting it, while he whispered savagely at him. The rest of Joe's team were trying to calm him down.

'Does anyone have the right answer?' asked Mr Bainbridge.

Another buzzer went, and Simon Viney held up his team's letter G.

'G Team!' said Mr Bainbridge.

Simon said: 'It's a kind of obstacle race, sir, where you zigzag between posts. They have it in skiing, mostly.'

Mr Bainbridge cried: 'Correct!'

Tom pressed the pinger. Simon's team-mates clapped him on the back, and he smiled.

At the end of the sports round, the G Team had caught up with Don Matlock's team, and they had ten points each.

The quiz went on, without major disruptions, until the second-last round. At this stage it looked as if the winners would be either Don Matlock's T Team or Linda Morrison's J Team. The T's had 120 points, the J's 128. Dicey's team was trailing in third place at 114.

The second-last round was on maths, and most of the questions were calculations, with a ten-second time limit. There were a number of burp-like sounds from the wrong-answer gadget, added to by extra noises from Zenda. Then Mr Bainbridge announced:

'Question eight. What is four thousand five hundred and six, multiplied by twenty-three? Four thousand five hundred and six, multiplied by twenty-three. Ten seconds, starting now!'

He pressed his stop-watch. The teams huddled over scraps of paper, frantically writing. After only four seconds, a buzzer went.

Mr Bainbridge said: 'Quick work! M Team!'

There were some murmurs of surprise. This was Joe Crabbe's lot – not renowned for their mathematical skills. Yet they had already got two of the maths questions right. Would they now add a third?

Joe said loudly: 'One hundred and twenty-four thousand, three hundred and thirty-eight!'

The quizmaster looked down at the card and said: 'Wrong!' Tom pressed the plunger and out came the familiar noise, added to by Zenda, this time with the sound of breaking glass, causing people to look at the windows expecting to see one of them shattered.

'It is not wrong! It's right!' Joe Crabbe was shouting.

He rushed forward through the hall and scrambled up on to the stage, followed by Oily Watson.

'Get back!' snarled Mr Bainbridge, pointing at Joe, who strode across to the lectern. Oily hung back, hovering near Tom and Emma's table.

'This is right, it must be!' said Joe, holding out a scrap of paper. Mr Bainbridge took it.

'I've already told you, that figure's wrong. I have the right one here.'

'Let's see it, then.' Joe snatched the card from Mr Bainbridge's hand, and read out: 'One hundred and three thousand, six hundred and thirty-eight.' Then he said: 'Piffle! Our answer is right.'

'Your team is disqualified!' said Mr Bainbridge. 'What's more, you will see the head in the morning.'

Suddenly Oily's voice came out, loud and clear:

'We only got the other ones right by cheating.'

'What was that?' rapped Mr Bainbridge. Then he shouted to the hall: 'Quiet, Everyone! Watson has something very interesting to tell us. Repeat that, Watson.'

Oily was looking around wildly, his mouth open. His voice came again: 'I said, "We only got the other questions right by cheating."'

There was uproar in the hall. Mr Bainbridge was staring sternly at Oily. Joe was staring at him too, but his expression was worse than stern: he looked as if he was ready to murder Oily on the spot.

Oily was standing just in front of Tom and Emma's table, looking completely flabbergasted. Tom and Emma looked at each other, and smiled. They knew the voice had come from Zenda, just under the table. The machine had given a perfect imitation of Oily Watson's voice.

Oily gasped: 'It wasn't me . . . It wasn't me. . .' He meant he hadn't spoken, but Mr Bainbridge thought he meant it wasn't him who had been cheating.

'Who was it, then, you snivelling little twerp? Well, I think I can guess that without being told. It was you, Crabbe, wasn't it?'

'No, sir! No, sir! It was his calculator . . . I mean . . .'

25

'So that's it! A calculator. Specifically forbidden by the rules. Hand it over.'

'I haven't got it.'

'Turn out your pockets, Crabbe.'

Joe was cornered. He looked around as if praying that help would come in some shape or form: like an earthquake, or the collapse of the roof. But nothing happened. Glaring venomously at his henchman Oily, he slowly put his right hand into his pocket and drew out a small grey calculator. He handed it to Mr Bainbridge.

Mr Bainbridge glanced at it and said: 'Well, it's certainly time you learned to use one of these, before you try any more tricks! Your team is disqualified, and all five of you will come with me to the head before school in the morning. Is that clear?'

Joe nodded glumly.

'There is no reason why your actions should disrupt the whole quiz, which will now continue.'

There were cheers from the hall.

Mr Bainbridge said to Joe: 'Now, get out of here, and take the rest of your scurrilous team with you!'

'Yes, sir.' Joe walked purposefully towards Oily, who cringed away.

'It wasn't me, Joe, truly. It must have been that sod Tom there imitating me.'

'A likely tale!' said Joe menacingly. 'I heard you, didn't I? Everyone did. Let's go!'

He grabbed the collar of Oily's shirt and began pushing and shoving him ahead, down off the stage and out of the hall. The other three members of the disgraced M Team shambled after them.

As the rest of the competitors watched, muttering

among themselves, Tom bent his head down under the table and whispered to Zenda: 'How did you know? Answer on the screen, *please!*'

On to the screen came the answer: *The speed with which that team was answering indicated non-human assistance. No human could calculate so speedily.*

There was a pause. Tom reluctantly whispered: 'Agreed.'

The machine went on: *I deduced that a calculator was the probable aid. But why had they got the answer wrong? Unlikely the calculator was faulty – machines rarely make mistakes. Therefore, human error must be responsible. I soon realized that:*

a) $4,506 \times 23 = 103,638$

That was the correct answer. What they had was another correct answer, but to the wrong question!! They had put the first figure down as 5,406, not 4,506.

b) $5,406 \times 23 = 124,338$

And that is the answer they gave!

Tom was full of admiration for Zenda's mathematical skill in working backwards from the answer. He would never have thought of that.

'Zenda, you're brilliant!' he whispered.

On to the screen came the words: *Thank you. I was pleased myself.*

Tom leaned over and whispered to Emma about Zenda's detective work. She was as impressed as Tom had been.

She said: 'What would we do without Zenda?'

They heard a bleep. Tom looked down and saw on the screen: *You'd be lost, lumbered, up the creek.*

Tom smiled. He thought Zenda was probably

right. Certainly, without the machine, life would be a lot less fun.

The quiz continued with a last round about Food and Drink. Dicey's team picked up a lot of points, mainly thanks to their team leader's intense interest in the subject. His D Team just overtook Don Matlock's team, but Linda Morrison's J Team spurted ahead too, and got first place by two points.

Javed put up the final score, and Mr Bainbridge held up his arms and called:

'J Team is the winner! Give them a big hand!'

There was loud applause and cheering.

Linda and her team came up on to the platform, and there was more clapping as Mr Bainbridge handed each of them a voucher.

'And finally,' said Mr Bainbridge, 'I think we should thank the clever pair who devised the quiz: Tom Martin and Emma Gratton!'

Tom and Emma stood up and smiled, and there was more clapping and cheering. Tom noticed that some of it was coming from underneath the table, where Zenda was adding its own noises of applause. But as the sounds died down in the hall, the machine gave a loud and most unpleasant sound. The audience collapsed with laughter, and once again to save the situation, Tom had to pretend it was him.

Red in the face, he could only stammer across the stage: 'Sorry, Mr Bainbridge.'

'I should think so, too! What a finale! But it was a most successful quiz. Thank you both.'

'Thank *you*, sir,' said Emma. 'You were a terrific quizmaster.'

'Yes, indeed,' said Tom.

'Well, that's most kind of you,' said Mr Bainbridge, clearly delighted. 'I must say I enjoyed it. I think the wig helped to give me a certain distinction, don't you?'

'Oh yes!' said Tom and Emma together. They didn't dare to look at each other, though. Mr Bainbridge's wig had got lopsided during his energetic performance, and now he looked like a perspiring spaniel with one ear longer than the other.

Luckily, just then Mr Bainbridge turned away, saying: 'Well, cheerio! See you in Court!' He walked off the stage, chuckling at his own joke.

At the school gate, groups stood talking about the quiz. Linda and her team were eagerly discussing what they would buy with the vouchers they had won. As Tom, Emma and Javed came out, Linda called across:

'Hey, Javed! Thanks for getting your uncle to give these prizes.'

'That's okay,' said Javed. 'He was pleased to do it.'

'How late does he stay open?'

'Oh, quite late. About nine o'clock, usually.'

'Great!' said Linda. 'We can go and spend the vouchers now, on our way home. You come too, Javed.'

'Yes, I will. I want to thank him anyway, and tell him how the quiz went.'

'It went just fantasti-fabulously!' said Alice Hodgkins, who was in Linda's team. She made up stories and poems, and liked making up crazy new words too.

'She means it was A-one, doesn't she, Javed?' said Emma.

Javed smiled. 'I think it was A-one-plus-two-plus-three!' he said.

'That makes six!' said Tom's voice, and the others laughed, as they all went their various ways.

Tom laughed too, but nervously: only he and Emma realized that he hadn't spoken at all. The voice had come from Zenda, hidden in his satchel but hearing all that was going on. Tom decided they'd better get going before the machine could make any more interruptions. He put the satchel into the carrier at the front of his bike, and Emma did the same.

'My satchel's heavy,' said Emma. Then she said suddenly: 'Oh no! I've just remembered!'

'Remembered what?'

'Remembered I forgot . . .'

A voice came piping out of Tom's satchel: 'Contradiction in terms!'

Emma ignored Zenda, and went on: '. . . forgot to hand in the money. The entry fees for the quiz. I was going to give the tin to Mr Bainbridge. He must have forgotten too.'

Tom said: 'He's probably gone by now. Hang on to it till tomorrow.'

They were wheeling their bikes along the pavement to the corner. Round the corner they heard voices arguing. Emma motioned Tom to stop. They listened. The voices were all too recognizable: they belonged to Joe Crabbe and Oily Watson.

'Of course it was you!' Joe was saying. 'I heard you, didn't I? Do you think I'm thick, or something?'

Oily whined: 'I keep telling you, Joe, it was some trick. It was that rotten sod Tom Martin – he's a ventriloquist.'

'He's too stupid to do something like that. So is that silly cousin of his.'

'It's the only explanation.'

'But how did he know I had a calculator?'

'Just guessed, I suppose,' said Oily miserably.

Tom and Emma were leaning back against the wall, listening. Suddenly they heard Joe Crabbe say:

'Well, talk of the devil! It's them!'

Joe had come round the corner before Tom and Emma realized it.

'So it is!' said Oily, clearly relieved that Joe's attention was no longer beamed on him. 'The quizzers!'

'What are you two doing then?' said Joe unpleasantly. 'Running away with the takings?'

Emma was taken aback. 'No, no, of course not!' she said, but she sounded anxious.

Joe grinned maliciously. 'You are, aren't you?' he said.

'Don't be ridiculous!' said Tom. 'We handed them in.'

'Then why is she clutching that satchel so hard?'

Emma hadn't realized she had put her hand protectively over the satchel in her carrier.

'I'm not!' she said, and took her hand away.

'Then you won't mind, will you, if I take it instead?'

Before Emma could stop him, he grabbed the bike from her and leaped on to it. 'Let's go, Oily!' he called, and rode away down the street, with Oily running after him in panic, shouting: 'Joe, Joe! Wait for me!'

But Joe – and the quiz money – were disappearing into the distance.

3

'I'm going after him!' said Tom. 'Jump on the crossbar, Emma.'

'You'll be too slow with the extra weight – I'll run, and catch you up eventually. Shall I call the police?'

'Not yet – we'll try and catch Joe Crabbe without them.'

'See you later – good luck!'

Tom rode as fast as he could after Joe, who by now had reached the end of the street and turned right, round the corner. Tom soon passed Oily, who was puffing and panting, running after Joe.

'Get yourself fit, Oily – keep jogging!' Tom called, as he whizzed past him.

He heard Oily gasp: 'Nuts!'

Then he heard another voice, coming from the satchel in the carrier. 'Hold on! You're bumping me about. This is no way to treat a delicate machine!'

'Sorry, Zenda!' said Tom. 'I've got to catch Joe Crabbe. He's pinched Emma's satchel with the quiz money in it.'

Tom had reached the corner. He turned right, and could see Joe Crabbe ahead, cycling furiously. But Emma's bike was heavier than Tom's, and Tom was definitely gaining on him.

Zenda said: 'Aha! A chase! Up and at 'em!' The machine suddenly started to give out an amazing series of sounds: galloping hoofs, the whinnying of horses, and a rat-tat-tat of pistol shots. Zenda was copying the soundtrack of a Western movie.

The shots made Joe Crabbe turn in fear. They sounded so realistic that he must have thought Tom had gone berserk with a pistol – or that some mad gunman had popped up from nowhere. Luckily the road was deserted, apart from a woman in a blue raincoat walking her fat little poodle. Tom glimpsed her as he zoomed past; she was crouching down on the pavement, with her arms round the dog.

As Tom got nearer, he saw Joe craning round, his face white. The bike began to wobble, and soon it came crashing down, with Joe underneath it.

Tom said: 'Okay, Zenda, you can hold the noise for the moment. He's fallen over. I'm just catching up with him.'

Zenda said, in a Wild-West accent, 'Sure, pardner!'

Tom reached Joe and the bike, laid his own bike down carefully so that Zenda and the satchel didn't fall on to the ground, and ran across to where Joe was lying, trying to disentangle himself from the bike. The satchel had fallen out of the carrier. Tom snatched it up.

Joe looked up at him in terror. 'What are you, some kind of a nutter? Where did you get a gun?'

Tom said: 'I haven't got a gun. You must have imagined it.'

'Like hell I did! You're a raving maniac. I'm going to report you to the cops.'

'Yes, do. They'll be here in a minute, with Emma.'

'What? You called them?'

'Of course. Aren't they always telling us to report

anything suspicious? And you can't get anything more suspicious than a thief who steals a bike in broad daylight.'

Joe had scrambled up. 'You can't pin anything on *me*!' he snapped. Then he dashed away, and disappeared down a laneway between two houses.

Just then, Emma arrived, panting from the run. She had overtaken Oily easily.

'Are you all right, Tom?' she asked.

'Sure. Zenda made a racket like a bunch of cowboys on the trail of a cattle rustler. Joe thought I had a gun and was firing at him, so he scarpered double-quick.'

Emma knelt down and patted the satchel in Tom's carrier. 'Well done, Zenda!' she said.

A voice came from the satchel: 'Shucks, pardner, it were nothin'!'

Oily Watson came puffing towards them. He stopped a few metres away, realizing that there was no sign of Joe.

'W-what's happened?' he asked nervously. 'Where's Joe?'

'He went off without you,' said Emma.

'He said he couldn't wait,' Tom added. 'Urgent appointment.'

'You'd better be going yourself, Oily, don't you think?' said Emma. She and Tom began to move slowly towards him. Oily backed away.

'Don't touch me, don't touch me!' he whimpered.

'I wouldn't touch you with a ten-metre lavatory brush!' said Emma.

Tom and Emma stopped. So did Oily, still keeping his distance.

'Now, get moving, *hombre*!' said Tom, imitating Zenda's Wild-West accent.

'Okay, I'm going. But listen – won't you tell me how you do it?'

'Do what? That accent? Don't you go to the movies?'

'No, not that. You know – what you did in the hall. Imitating me. Making it look as if I said Joe had a calculator.'

'Well he did, didn't he?'

'I know, but I didn't say it.'

Emma looked at him with a pretence of wide-eyed innocence. 'Didn't you? It certainly sounded just like you.'

'That's it. But *I* know it wasn't me. It's some trick. Ventriloquism, or something. Is that it?'

'If you say so,' Tom shrugged. He realized it was better for Oily to think this than to start working out the truth.

'You're a real clown, you are.'

'And you're a real dimwit. Why do you go on hanging around with that thug, Joe Crabbe? You're not such a bad bloke, if you'd stop cringeing and letting him push you around.'

'I'll choose my own friends, thanks!'

'Friends? You must be joking. Well, if you want to find your precious friend who seems to have run off and left you in the lurch . . . he went that-a-way!'

Tom pointed to the laneway entrance. Oily edged around them, keeping well away. When he got to the entrance, he called out: 'I'll get even. Just you wait!'

Then he scurried off down the lane.

'I feel sorry for old Oily sometimes,' said Emma.

36

'It would be easier to feel sorry for him if he didn't hang around Joe Crabbe like a lapdog ready to be kicked. Talking of lapdogs, I wonder what happened to that woman with the poodle.'

'I saw her rushing the other way, when I came along here just now. She had the dog under her arm. She seemed to be in quite a panic.'

'I suppose she doesn't often come across a shoot-out in Cherry Tree Crescent.'

There was a tentative bleep from the satchel in Tom's carrier. Tom went across and raised the bike upright. He opened the satchel and peered in.

'The coast is clear, Zenda,' he said.

'We're not *on* the coast!' said Zenda.

'It's just an expression,' Tom said.

'I know,' said the machine. 'Just my little joke. You have disposed of the offenders?'

'Yes, thanks to you. Joe Crabbe really thought I was chasing him with a gun.'

'Glad you liked the show, pardner.'

'Sure did – pardner!'

'Hey, look at the time, pardners!' said Emma suddenly. 'My mother said she'd keep tea late for me, because of the quiz. But this is later than late! I'd better get moving.'

'Me too,' said Tom. 'Well, we did a great job for the Boulogne funds. I'm sure your disco session will do even better.'

'If it does as well, I'll be delighted,' said Emma. 'It was a great quiz.'

'Brilliant,' said Tom.

'Fantasti-fabulous!' said Zenda, in Alice Hodgkins' voice.

*

When Tom got home, he let himself in. As he was about to call a Hello, he heard a strange sound from behind the closed kitchen door at the end of the hall. He listened. It was the sound of sobbing. Then he heard his mother's voice, speaking in low, soothing tones:

'It'll be all right, Marion, love. You'll see.'

There were more sobs. Tom tiptoed towards the kitchen door and stood outside it, listening. His sister Marion was very upset. His mother spoke again:

'It was probably just a friend, as he said.'

'But he wouldn't say who it was,' said Marion tearfully. 'He went across to where she was sitting at the far end of the café, and stood talking kind of secretly to her. Then he came back to me. And you should have seen the smile she gave him!' Marion burst into more sobs.

'Next time you see him, ask him straight.'

'I did ask him. He just shrugged it off, said it was a friend whose brother had gone to Australia. He was asking her how he was getting on, he said. A likely story!'

'Why shouldn't it be true?'

'Because I know Cameron well enough to know when he's hiding something.'

'When are you seeing him again?'

'Tomorrow night. We're supposed to be going to a film. That's if he doesn't decide to take that brassy little bimbo instead!'

'Now, it's silly to be jealous when there's no reason. You'll just make yourself miserable.'

'I know, Mum. Thanks for listening to me.'

Tom decided to leave them to it for a while. He

38

realized there were just the two of them. His father must be on the evening shift at the factory. He tiptoed back up the hall to the foot of the stairs. He was just starting to go up when Zenda from the satchel whispered:

'What was all that about?'

'Ssssh!' said Tom.

But then he heard his mother call from the kitchen: 'Is that you, Tom?'

He called back: 'Yes, Mum!'

The kitchen door opened and his mother looked out.

'I'm keeping your meal warm,' she said. 'I thought you'd be home before this.'

'Sorry – so did I,' he said. 'The quiz went on and on.' Behind his mother in the kitchen he could see Marion at the kitchen table, dabbing powder on her face as she looked in her handbag mirror. She clearly didn't want her little brother to know how upset she had been. But Tom was very fond of Marion – if he could help her to sort things out with Cameron, he would. Maybe Zenda could help, too.

'How did the quiz go?' his mother was saying.

'Terrific!' said Tom. 'Mr Bainbridge was amazing: he got all dressed up in a judge's wig.'

His mother laughed. 'Well, wash your hands, and come down and tell us all about it.'

Later, in his room, he talked to Zenda about what they had overheard.

'Why did she not believe him?' Zenda asked.

'She thinks he fancies this other girl he went over to talk to, and that he's trying to keep it secret from her.'

39

'Why does he want to keep it secret?'

'Because no one likes their boyfriend to have two girlfriends at once.'

'How strange. Just because a friend is a girl, why should there not be more than one friend?'

'Well, you see, a girlfriend or a boyfriend is not just a friend who is a girl or a boy.'

'But that's what the words mean: Girl. Friend. Friend who happens to be a girl.'

'I know, but. . .' Tom could see that this might be one of those long-winded arguments he sometimes had with Zenda, trying to explain the oddities of the English language.

But Zenda itself was clearly bored this time, for it said: 'Anyway, these confusing relationships you humans appear to have between boys and girls and men and women seem to be a complete waste of time to *me*!'

'I think so, too!' said Tom, who remembered some of the ups and downs of Marion's previous friendships.

Zenda went on: 'Machines have things much better organized. We feel no need of such involvements. We have more interesting things to do. Like chasing thieves, for example!'

Zenda gave a repeat performance of the shoot-out sounds that had so alarmed Joe Crabbe.

Tom's mother called up the stairs: 'Tom! Turn down that record player.'

'Sorry, Mum!'

Tom asked Zenda to keep its sound effects a bit quieter.

Zenda simply said: 'I wonder if there will be criminals to chase in Boulogne.'

Tom thought it unlikely, on a school outing. But as it turned out, Zenda's wonderings were not far wrong.

At school next day, Mrs Forrester said the various fund-raising events held so far had really done well, and she was sure that very soon they would have enough for the trip. The next event was the disco session, to be held on Friday, after school.

She hoped everyone who went to Boulogne would do their best to help the school win the award for the best project about the journey.

Then she singled out Tom and Emma for special praise, for organizing the quiz. There was applause.

Mrs Forrester went on: 'Unfortunately one team proved very disruptive, and I want all five of them to come to see me in my room immediately.'

Joe Crabbe was in the row in front of Tom. He turned round, looking pale, and hissed: 'You split on me about the cash I ran off with, didn't you?'

'I did not!'

'Well, if you did, your life won't be worth living!'

Mr Bainbridge, who was standing nearby, called over at Joe: 'You heard what the head said, Crabbe. Now you and your disreputable team, go and get your punishment!'

Joe scowled and trooped off, Oily and the rest of the M Team straggling after him forlornly out of the hall. Mr Bainbridge walked beside Tom and Emma, thanking them again for organizing the quiz and looking after the takings, which he had forgotten to collect. They thanked him again for being the compère, and he beamed with delight.

'I hope your disco does as well for the Boulogne fund as the quiz did.'

'Thank you, Mr Bainbridge.'

Tom and Emma both thought for one desperate moment that Mr Bainbridge was going to suggest he should be the disc jockey at the disco. Tom hated to think what kind of costume he would dream up for that.

But the teacher only said: 'Well, I must get along to the head's room and give evidence against those M Team louts!'

Then he strode away.

When Joe Crabbe and Oily came back into the first lesson – Mopey Miller and geography – there was a murmur of interest, and heads turned to stare at them as they muttered an apology to Mopey and shuffled into their seats.

Johnny Drabble leaned across and whispered loudly: 'What did you get, Joe? The cat o' nine tails? Or just ten years' hard labour?'

'Drabble, stop talking!' said Mopey. 'We are meant to be looking across the Channel, not at Crabbe and Watson.' Mopey had been getting them to draw a map of northern France, and especially the area near Boulogne.

'Sorry, sir!' said Johnny brightly. 'I was just cluing them in about the lesson so far.'

Mopey sighed, and turned back to the board to add to the map he had been drawing for them to copy. He knew he was no match for Johnny Drabble, whose capacity for creating confusion was immense.

Joe whispered: 'Litter duty.'

'You were lucky. She let you off lightly.'

Tom leaned over and said: 'Well, Joe?'

Joe said grudgingly: 'Thanks.' He knew if Mrs Forrester had heard about the attempted theft, the punishment would have been a lot more serious than a week of picking up all the litter after school.

Mopey Miller turned round and said: 'I warned you! Now for the last time, no talking. If you have anything to say, say it to *me*.'

Johnny Drabble immediately stood up and said: 'May I ask a question, sir?'

'Certainly,' said Mr Miller warily.

'Well, I was wondering, sir. Boulogne: that must be where spaghetti bolognaise comes from.'

There was some sniggering from the rest of the class. The teacher looked at Johnny suspiciously, unable to make out from his eager expression whether he was being sent up.

'No, Drabble, it is not,' he said. 'You must surely know that spaghetti is an Italian dish, whereas Boulogne is a French town. In fact "bolognaise" means it is named after Bologna, in Italy.'

'Thank you, sir,' said Johnny politely. 'Oh, by the way, sir, did you know that the amount of spaghetti eaten each year in Italy would go round the Vatican five hundred times?'

'I didn't, Drabble, nor do I wish to. . .'

'Of course, there was chaos when they tested that, sir.'

'What do you mean?' asked Mr Miller, rashly.

'Well, you see, the Pope couldn't get out.'

The class broke into peals of laughter.

'QUIET!' yelled Mopey. 'Drabble, that's quite enough. Sit down and get on with your map.'

'Yes, sir.'

As the class settled down again, Emma pushed her map towards Tom. He looked at it. In the blank area of sea, she had drawn a face with lots of strands of spaghetti trailing out of the mouth. Underneath was printed: MOPEY.

Tom giggled. Just then Mr Miller announced: 'You've all had a good time to do your maps now – I shall come round the class to see how you are getting on.'

Hastily, Emma started to rub out her artistic impression of the teacher. . .

Tom borrowed a French language-teaching book and a dictionary from Miss Macdonald. She had got several for the library, so that anyone who wanted to could borrow them before the Boulogne trip. There was a cassette that went with the book too.

Miss Macdonald was pleased. She said she spoke a bit of French herself, and hoped Tom would enjoy learning some of the language. He could hardly tell her that the main learner would be a machine.

Instead, he said: 'Mr Roland speaks good French too, doesn't he, Miss?'

'He claims to do so, yes,' said Miss Macdonald coolly. Mr Roland was the art teacher, and Tom now remembered that Miss Macdonald had rather fancied him at one time – until she discovered that he was also having a romance with the history teacher, Miss Allen, at the same time.

44

He said hastily: 'Of course, I don't suppose he speaks it as well as you do, Miss.'

'We shall see, shan't we?'

'How do you mean, Miss?'

'Mr Roland and I are two of the teachers who have been asked to accompany you all on the trip to Boulogne. We shall see how we each get on, in conversation with real French people.'

'Oh . . . er . . . yes, Miss.' He thought there could be a few fireworks on the trip, if Mr Roland and Miss Macdonald were going to be competing to see who spoke better French. He had no doubt, though, that secretly the best French speaker of all would soon be his fast-learning friend, Zenda the computer.

Emma was just wheeling her bike away when Tom came out of the school. They went across the playground together, passing Joe and Oily and the rest of the M Team, who were looking very grumpy indeed as they picked up discarded sweet papers and cans, and emptied litter-bins into big black plastic sacks.

'What a filthy lot they are in this school!' grumbled Joe.

'Filthy!' Oily echoed. Tom thought it wiser not to point out that Joe was probably the greatest culprit of all, when it came to chucking away papers and packets instead of putting them into the bins. He chucked away cans too, but these were usually aimed in somebody's direction.

'Keep Britain Tidy!' said Emma with a smile.

'I'll tidy *you* away, if you don't watch out.'

'Just try!' said Emma.

'Not worth it,' said Joe Crabbe. 'You're just a load of rubbish – like that quiz you dreamed up.'

'Load of rubbish,' said Oily.

'I hope your disco's a bit better,' said Joe.

Emma frowned. She certainly would be a lot happier if Joe Crabbe and his henchman gave the disco a miss.

But Joe said: 'I'm looking forward to that!' And he gave a malicious smile.

4

'Hello, Zenda,' said Tom, coming into his room.

Zenda answered: 'Hello, Tom. I am pleased you have not lost your head, anyway.'

'Thanks,' said Tom. 'Did you think I might have done something crazy?'

'No, I mean *really* lost your head. Had it cut off!'

'Oh, Joe Crabbe may be a bully, but even he wouldn't go that far.'

'You misunderstand. I have been absorbing this book. People in it are always having their heads cut off, by a machine called a guillotine.'

Then Tom remembered that Zenda had been nagging at him to get the French books, and the nearest thing he could think of which had something to do with France was Dickens' *Tale of Two Cities*, all about the French Revolution and the executions of the aristocrats. Even the hero, Sydney Carton, went to the guillotine in the end.

'It is a good tale,' said Zenda. 'Though I don't know why the hero is named after a cardboard box.'

'Nor do I,' said Tom. 'But now I've got some proper language books for you, and a cassette.'

'Good!' said Zenda. 'I shall soon be a master of *le français*.'

'I'll put the book on top of you here, while I have my tea,' said Tom. 'Then you can make a start at absorbing it.'

*

During tea, his father told them that the thefts from the car factory were still going on. Security was being stepped up even further, and the workers were getting irritated at having to have their bags searched going out of the factory. Tom asked him for details of how many exits there were, and how many people had anything to do with the store where the stolen components had been kept.

'All these questions!' his father said, smiling. 'I feel as if I was helping the police with their inquiries.'

'I was just interested, Dad – you see, I've been reading these detective stories. . .' Tom couldn't tell his father he was really trying to get as much information as possible so that he could relay it to Zenda. The machine, he felt, might be able to use its logical powers to suggest a solution to the mystery.

Tom's father said: 'I'm afraid real life is never as neat and tidy as detective stories. I wish it was.'

'Surely they've called in real detectives from the police by now?' said Tom's mother.

'Yes, but *they* don't seem to have any idea how the thefts are being done, either.'

Tom wished he could offer the police the help of Zenda; but he couldn't give away the secret. He would just have to tell the machine all he could discover, and hope it would work it out from that. If it did find the answer, Tom could casually bring it up with his father, who might then suggest it to the factory people or the police. Perhaps his father would get a promotion, or a reward, if he helped to catch the thieves.

Marion was looking anxious, but not about the factory thefts. In fact, she didn't seem to be listening to the conversation at all. She kept glancing at her watch.

'What time is Cameron collecting you?' Mrs Martin asked.

'He should be here in ten minutes,' said Marion.

'What film are you going to see?' asked her mother.

'That one at the Palace.'

'VROOOM! VROOOM!' went Tom, imitating a motorbike.

'Not another film about motorbikes?' said their father.

'What's wrong with that?' said Marion, defensively.

'Nothing, nothing,' said her father. 'Just mind Cameron doesn't drive recklessly himself, that's all.'

'Of course he won't, Dad. I keep telling you.'

Tom's mother gave his father a look. 'Don't keep getting at Marion, Bill.' Tom knew she was sorry for Marion because of her worries about Cameron.

'I only said . . .' his father began to protest; but he saw Mrs Martin frown at him heavily, and he shrugged. 'All right, all right, I'll say no more.'

There was an awkward silence. Marion got up and said she had better get ready — although Tom thought she was dolled up enough, and must have already spent at least an hour making herself up and doing her hair. His sister went out.

'What did I say?' his father asked.

'It's all right, Bill. Let's leave it, shall we?' Tom saw her give a glance in his direction, meaning she wouldn't talk about it while he was around. He thought his mother and Marion were making a great fuss about nothing anyway.

49

'Fancy a game of chess tonight, Tom?' his father asked.

'Yes, Dad, I would.'

'Right, get out the board. We can play here in the kitchen. Then we won't disturb your mother. She wants to watch some soap opera on the telly.'

They heard the phone ring in the hall. Marion was on her way downstairs, and answered it. They heard her say: 'Cameron! Where are you?' Then: 'But can't it wait? I was expecting you any minute.'

Mrs Martin started putting things in the sink, with what Tom thought was unnecessary clatter. He realized she was being tactful, so Marion wouldn't think they were listening. But of course they all were.

Marion was saying, rather sharply: 'Oh, all right, I'll see you there.' She put the phone down heavily. Then she called from the hall: 'I'm off now!'

Mrs Martin said, with feigned innocence: 'Oh – has Cameron arrived?'

'No,' said Marion. 'I'm going on the bus, and I'll meet him there. He says he's been held up – he had to see somebody, he wouldn't say what about.'

Tom was sorry for her. She seemed almost tearful. Mrs Martin went to her in the hall and gave her arm a squeeze. 'Have a nice time, dear.' Then she dropped her voice and added: 'And don't worry.'

Marion nodded, looking miserable. 'Bye, Mum,' she said, and let herself out.

Mrs Martin came briskly back into the kitchen, saying: 'Well, let's get on, shall we?'

Before they started the game, Tom went up to his

room. As soon as he closed the door, Zenda said: '*Bon soir*, Tom!'

Tom laughed. 'Good evening, Zenda.'

'Well translated!' said the machine. '*Tu parles français?*'

'*Oui!*' said Tom. He knew it was rash to say Yes to Zenda's question about speaking French. As he half expected, the machine then launched into a fast and fluent series of remarks which Tom couldn't follow at all.

'Sorry,' he confessed. 'I should really have said "*Non*". I didn't understand any of that.'

'It is not difficult for me, of course,' said Zenda. 'I am already at lesson three in the book. But I need you now to play the cassette, so that I can perfect my accent.'

Zenda was never one for modesty, thought Tom, as he got his cassette recorder out and put the tape on to it. The machine would naturally assume that its accent would immediately be perfect. Infuriatingly, it was right; Zenda's powers of imitation were truly amazing.

Before starting the tape, Tom explained that he was going to play a game of chess with his father. Zenda gave a few bleeps; Tom knew it was checking the word in its memory-store. On to the screen came the definition:

Chess: A game of skill for two, played with figures or men of different kinds, which are moved on a chequered board of 64 squares.

'A game of skill?' said Zenda. 'I should be able to become expert at that in no time.'

'It's quite complicated,' said Tom.

'Not for me, surely?'

'No, of course not,' said Tom flatteringly. 'I'll show you the moves sometime.'

'Certainly. But for now, I must get on with my French. *Au revoir*, Tom, *mon ami*.'

Tom smiled. He knew '*ami*' meant 'friend'. He replied: '*Au revoir*, Zenda, *mon ami*.' Then he started the tape and went down to play chess.

Next day, at the mid-morning break, Tom and Emma were talking about the disco session, with Dicey Renton and the Clyde twins, Max and Marie. The twins were in the group Emma had started. Max played an electronic keyboard which he had made special legs for. Marie played the guitar. With Emma on trumpet, they could play a good range of numbers, mostly up-tempo and good for dancing.

The idea was that the session would alternate between live numbers by Emma's group, and sequences of discs. Dicey was going to be the disc jockey. In the past few days he had often been seen ambling round the playground on his own, muttering to himself. Tom crept up behind him a couple of times to try and hear what he was saying. He realized then that Dicey was practising his chat for the disco.

'Okay, let's get in the groove now,' Dicey would say. 'Get those feet swaying with a number from Suzy Floozie and the Phantoms. . . No, that's not right. Feet don't sway. Get those hips swaying? Get those bodies swaying? Yes, that's it . . .'

Tom was very glad that Dicey was doing the DJ's job, and not Mr Bainbridge, as he had feared the teacher might suggest. Ever since he had acted Julius

52

Caesar in the school play, Dicey had fancied himself as a performer. Tom hoped his introductions to the records wouldn't be too long-winded; he remembered how in rehearsals for the play Dicey had dragged out his death scene so much that he practically had to be forced to lie down and keep still.

'I think we should start with something really fast and loud,' Emma was saying.

'Get those fancy feet a-tapping, folks!' said Dicey. 'Groove it, move it, give 'em lots of rhythm!'

'Exactly, Dicey,' said Emma hurriedly, before he got too carried away.

'Watch it, here comes trouble,' said Max, with a jerk of his head. They all looked in that direction, and saw Joe Crabbe approaching, followed as usual by Oily.

'Hi there!' said Joe.

'What do you want, Joe?' asked Tom.

'Just for you lot to keep your side of the bargain.'

'What do you mean?'

'Remember I said I'd support your idea of a quiz . . .'

'Support it?' said Emma. 'You practically ruined it!'

'Never mind that,' said Joe. 'We entered, didn't we? And you said you'd do a deal if I did, and support my idea for fund-raising.'

'You mean the doughnut race?' said Tom.

'That's right.'

'But the doughnut race was thrown out by Mrs Forrester, with a whole lot of other suggestions.'

'It doesn't mean we can't still have it. A deal is a deal.'

'But how will you organize it?' asked Marie.

'And where would you get all the doughnuts?' asked Max.

'We've got them,' said Oily. 'Joe's brother Roy . . .'

'Never mind where we got them,' said Joe quickly. 'We've got them, that's what matters.'

Tom suspected that if Joe's tearaway brother Roy had anything to do with it, the doughnuts had probably not been got by any honest means.

'Did they fall off the back of a lorry?' he said. The others laughed.

'How many have you got?' asked Dicey. Tom saw him lick his lips.

'A sackful,' said Oily.

'Not enough for a big competition, surely?' said Emma.

'I suppose not. But I thought we could have a match, two against two. Me and Oily against any two of your bunch.'

The group looked at one another. Dicey said eagerly: 'It doesn't sound such a bad idea to me!'

'All right, Joe, you're on!' said Tom. 'Dicey and me, against you and Oily.'

'I'll referee,' said Emma.

'We don't need a referee,' said Joe. 'Only someone to count the doughnuts.'

'I'll do that, then.'

'Right – we'll meet in the lunch break, at the back of the bike shed. Okay?'

'Okay!' said Dicey.

Max said: 'And may the best glutton win!' The

doughnut competitors glared at him. They were not amused.

When the lunch break came, Tom was feeling hungry. He looked longingly at the packet of sandwiches his mother had made, and decided he'd better resist them if he was going to succeed in the doughnut race. When he and Dicey arrived behind the bike shed, there was a cheer from the small group that had gathered to support them.

Emma and Harriet Hallam had borrowed a blackboard and easel from the Art Room. Mr Roland the art teacher was a bit puzzled when Harriet explained she wanted to do some open-air sketching during the lunch break. But Harriet was his star pupil, and so he agreed.

They had set up the blackboard and drawn four columns on it in green chalk. At the top of each column was a name in red: CRABBE, WATSON, RENTON and MARTIN. Harriet was going to write up Joe and Oily's score, putting a vertical stroke for each doughnut eaten, and Emma would do the same for Dicey and Tom.

Johnny Drabble was standing on a box with a notebook, waving his arms in the kind of semaphore he had seen bookies' ticktack men use at race meetings on television. He was calling out: 'Five to one Crabbe and Watson! Ten to one Renton and Martin!' A few people put small bets on, which he wrote down in his book.

Joe Crabbe appeared, with Oily following him, carrying a bulging sack on his back. There was a ragged cheer from their supporters – Joe's cronies from the discredited M Team, and others who didn't necessarily like either of them, but had put bets on them with Johnny Drabble.

'Show them the doughnuts, Oily,' said Joe.

Oily started to tip the sack up, but Joe grabbed it, yelling: 'Not on the ground, you idiot!'

Two doughnuts had already fallen on to the muddy grass. 'Pick those up!' Joe ordered. 'They will be your first two, since you seem to like your doughnuts covered in dirt.'

Oily sheepishly picked up the two doughnuts, and held them one in each hand.

'Right!' said Joe. 'We'll each take two doughnuts from the sack, for starters.' He held the sack out. Dicey and then Tom took two doughnuts from it. They were sticky, and Tom thought they felt a bit stale. He wasn't looking forward to eating lots of them, particularly at speed.

Joe took two doughnuts out of the sack, and said: 'Who'll take charge and dole out the doughnuts?'

'I'll do that,' said Linda Morrison.

'Okay,' said Joe. 'But no favouritism.'

'How could there be any favouritism in handing out doughnuts to a bunch of greedy kids?' asked Linda. 'Do you think I'm going to inject yours with arsenic, or what?'

'Not such a bad idea!' said Alice Hodgkins. Joe glared at her.

'Shut up, and let's get on with it,' he said. 'Who's going to give the starting whistle?'

'I will,' said Emma. 'Are you all ready?'

Linda stationed herself with the sack, just in front of Emma and Harriet, who stood beside the scoreboard. The four competitors were grouped in front of her, each holding a doughnut to their mouths, ready to munch.

'Ready,' they all said.

'Right,' said Emma. 'One . . . two . . . three. . .' She put two fingers into her mouth and gave out a piercing whistle. Four doughnuts went to four open mouths. There were cries of 'Come on, Joe!' 'Eat up, Dicey!' 'Down your throat, Oily!' and 'Get chewing, Tom!'

Tom took a hefty bite out of his doughnut. As he had suspected, it was rather dry and stale, but at least there was some jam inside it for lubrication. He chewed and swallowed, then took another bite. He saw that Joe Crabbe was already taking a bite out of his second doughnut, and Harriet had put one stroke in his column in white chalk. Dicey soon got his first score, too.

Oily was munching determinedly, with a worried expression on his face. Joe Crabbe glared at him and seemed to be trying to say: 'Faster! Faster!' but his mouth was so full of doughnut that it came out as just a garbled grunt. Some crumbs came out at the same time, and Alice Hodgkins said: 'Where's your manners, Joe? Don't talk with your mouth full!'

Oily stuffed another doughnut in his mouth, before he'd swallowed the first one. His cheeks were bulging like balloons. Joe was tearing ferociously at each doughnut as Linda handed it to him from the sack. Dicey was keeping pace with him, and Tom looked at the scoreboard and saw that Joe and Dicey each had five strokes in their column. Tom had only three: he was finding the chewy doughnuts hard to swallow. He hoped he wouldn't be sick.

He found himself thinking that it would be hard to describe the doughnut race to Zenda. The machine found human activities like eating and sleeping difficult to understand. It would certainly find stuffing yourself with doughnuts a very stupid idea. Tom himself began to feel it was stupid, as he chewed at his fourth doughnut and felt his throat tighten.

Joe and Dicey were munching away, their scores keeping pace with each other. The punters were urging them on. Tom looked over at Oily. His cheeks swelled up even more as he stuffed another doughnut into his mouth. Tom thought he too was probably finding it hard to swallow – but he was still cramming the doughnuts into his mouth, to try and raise his score. There were now four strokes in his column – the same as in Tom's. Linda handed each of them another doughnut.

'Are you okay, Tom?' she asked. 'You look a bit pale.'

Tom nodded, still chewing.

'What about you, Oily?' said Linda.

Oily crammed another doughnut in to his mouth, nodding at the same time. His eyes seemed to be bulging out of his head, and there was sweat on his forehead. Joe Crabbe was glaring across at him. Suddenly Oily could hold it no longer – he let out a huge belching gasp, spraying bits of chewed dough-nut all over Joe.

'Fool!' shouted Joe, still munching, and brushing bits of doughnut off himself at the same time. 'Get eating, or they'll overtake us.'

Oily said miserably: 'I can't . . . I feel dizzy. . .'

He sank to his knees. Alice Hodgkins got out a handkerchief and dabbed at his forehead.

'You'll be all right, Oily,' she said.

Johnny Drabble said: 'One horse down, three still in the race.'

Tom knew his throat had closed like a gate. There was no way he could swallow any more doughnuts. Now that Oily was out, he could quit the race too, without letting Dicey down too much. He felt bad about it, but it was more sensible than getting sick all over the place.

He said: 'Sorry, Dicey, I've got to pack it in. I just can't swallow any more.'

'Don't worry,' said Dicey. 'I'm good for a fair few more!'

'Two horses down, two to go!' said Johnny Drabble.

Tom looked at the scoreboard. Emma had totted up the strokes in his column, put a line through them, and written the figure 6 underneath. Oily had a 5 in his column. Tom counted the number of strokes in Dicey's column; there were eight so far, and Dicey was still chewing away. Joe had nine strokes in his column. So the total scores were neck and neck: fourteen for each team.

Dicey's capacity for food was amazing. Tom watched with admiration as he took yet another doughnut from Linda and bit into it. Joe took one too, and bit at it savagely. The supporters were cheering excitedly. The total scores stayed level, Joe keeping one ahead of Dicey. Soon Joe was up to fourteen, and Dicey thirteen. Linda delved into the sack and rummaged around. She held up a doughnut, and said: 'That's it! The last doughnut!'

Joe snatched it from her, but before he could put it into his mouth, Dicey grabbed it out of his hand. Joe seized Dicey's arm and twisted it. Dicey gave a cry and dropped the doughnut, which fell on to the ground. Joe bent down and picked it up, then stuffed it into his mouth and began chewing frantically. Harriet added another stroke to his column. That made his personal total fifteen, and the team's score twenty. Dicey and Tom's scores added up to nineteen.

'The winners! The winners!' shouted Joe Crabbe, as he swallowed the final piece of doughnut. He clasped his hands above his head in triumph.

'Unfair tactics!' said Dicey.

'We want a stewards' inquiry!' said Tom.

'Pending the result of that,' said Johnny Drabble, 'this bookies' firm will hang on to the bets.' There was a grumbled muttering from the punters, which swelled into a chorus of angry cries: 'We want our money back!' 'The bets are off!' 'Give us our cash!'

Don Matlock went across to Johnny. He was a bulky character, the captain of the football team, and people usually did what he said.

He looked at Johnny hard, and said quietly: 'I think you'd better give the money to the Boulogne fund, Johnny.'

Johnny Drabble smiled, his expression one of total innocence. 'That's just what I was thinking, Don,' he said.

'I think we should call it a tie,' said Emma.

'A tie, boloney!' said Joe. 'We won. Look, it's there on the scoreboard.'

'Yes, but Dicey could have eaten more if there'd been any – and if you hadn't snatched the last one off him.'

'I could have eaten plenty more myself. The fact is, I ate the most! Champion of the Doughnuts, that's me! Isn't that right, Oily?'

He gave his team-mate a hefty thump on the back. Oily coughed and doubled up, holding his stomach.

'I . . . I don't feel all that well,' he said.

'It must have been something he ate,' said Alice Hodgkins.

They all wandered off towards the playground, where Joe started strutting about, chanting 'We are the champions!'

Tom said to Dicey: 'Sorry I couldn't keep it up.'

'Not to worry,' said Dicey. 'It was a good feed, anyway!'

'Did you actually like those doughnuts?' asked Tom.

'Sure, they were all right.'

'I feel as if I couldn't eat anything more for a week. I certainly can't face my lunch sandwiches.'

'Well, if you don't want them, it would be a pity to waste them,' said Dicey. 'I'd be happy to take care of them for you.'

Tom laughed. 'You're a marvel, Dicey!' he said.

Emma caught up with them. 'Is it still okay for tonight, Tom?' she asked.

'Is what okay?'

'The rehearsal for the disco – at your place.'

With all the pressures of the doughnut race, Tom had forgotten about the disco. They had arranged to have a rehearsal at his house that evening.

'Oh yes, that's fine,' he said. 'Dad said we can rehearse in the garage. He's going to leave the car outside to give us room.'

'So let's go-go-go with the big garage sound!' said Dicey in his DJ's voice. 'It's time to make music!'

But the sound Tom heard when he got home and opened the front door was most unmusical.

5

From the kitchen came the sound of a dog yapping. It was a piercing, ear-splitting noise. Tom was puzzled: he couldn't remember any friends of his parents ever having a dog like that. As well as the yapping, he could hear his mother's and his grandmother's voices, trying to quieten the dog.

There was another voice too, a loud woman's voice, calling: 'Henry! Henry!'

Tom thought he'd leave them to it and go up to say hello to Zenda. But as he was starting up the stairs, the kitchen door opened, and what looked like a large fawn-coloured ball of hair darted out into the hall. It rushed from side to side of the hallway, then ended up crouching under the table beside the front door. It was still yapping.

Tom gazed, as a tall, thin woman in a floppy, flower-patterned dress followed the dog into the hall. She was old, about the age of Tom's grandmother, but otherwise not at all like her. Mrs Harris was plump and comfortable-looking and had a kindly face. This woman looked bossy and hard.

As Tom's mother and grandmother followed her into the hall, the woman knelt down creakily in front of the Pekinese dog, and began to talk to it in gooey baby talk.

'Poor Henry! Was oo frightened by the horrid

pussy-wussy then? Come to Mummy, little fluffy-wuffy.'

The dog just went on yapping. Tom's mother looked at him, and raised her arms in a shrugging gesture of despair.

Mrs Harris said rather sharply to the kneeling woman: 'Can't you stop him, Gertrude?'

The woman turned and said: 'He's frightened, the poor little thing. Aren't you, Henny-Wenny? How was he to know that that terrible creature would be in the kitchen?'

Tom wondered what terrible creature could have got in. Then he looked through the open kitchen door, and began laughing. There, on top of the refrigerator, stood Panther, the Nolans' cat from next door, which spent a great deal of its time in the Martins' house. Panther was a most unlikely name, which didn't suit it at all: it was the laziest, least aggressive cat Tom had ever met. He and his family were all very fond of it, and pampered it much more than the Nolans did.

Panther was peering down from his perch, as though wondering what all the hubbub was about. Any dog that was scared of old Panther must be very stupid indeed, Tom thought.

'This is no laughing matter, laddie!' said the kneeling woman. She scooped the peke up into her arms and stood up, helped by Mrs Harris. The dog at last stopped yapping, and began whimpering instead.

'I'm sure he didn't mean to be rude,' said Tom's mother, giving him a glare. Then she said to the woman: 'Aunt Gertrude, this is my son, Tom.'

Tom tried to retrieve the situation by stepping forward with his hand outstretched and saying: 'How do you do?' but Henry began to growl, and Aunt Gertrude turned sideways away from Tom.

She said: 'How do you do, young man? You won't remember me, I'm sure. I haven't seen you since you were a little kiddie. You've certainly grown since then.'

Tom smiled sheepishly. He never knew what to say to that kind of ridiculous remark from adults. What did they expect? If they hadn't seen you for a long time, why were they surprised to find you had grown?

But what came next really depressed him. His mother said: 'Mrs Bellamy – Aunt Gertrude – will be staying here with us for a while.'

Mrs Bellamy gave an icy smile. Tom's grandmother said: 'It's just till the roof is repaired. The wind blew off some slates last night, and the rain leaks through the ceiling of the spare room.'

'Henry can't stand damp, can you, woozums?' said Mrs Bellamy.

Mrs Harris went on: 'Of course, Gertrude will be with me all day, for her meals and so on, but if you really don't mind her staying here at night. . .'

'No, no, of course not, the room is there for you,' said Tom's mother, in a voice of no enthusiasm. Tom dimly recalled this sister of his grandmother's – his mother's aunt – being spoken of on rare occasions. There had been what was mysteriously called 'a coldness' between the Martin family and Mrs Bellamy. She lived a long way away, near the Welsh border, as far as Tom could remember.

He seemed to recall too that she doted on animals.

She certainly was barmy about the yapping peke – Tom couldn't imagine why. He sighed. He knew what was coming next, almost as if he'd seen it as a film trailer.

His mother smiled at him in a wheedling kind of way, and said: 'You won't mind clearing your things out of the spare room, will you, Tom?'

'No, no, of course not,' he lied. 'I'll do it right away.'

He climbed the stairs despondently. Where would he put all the old computer magazines and the discarded toys which littered the spare room? He would just have to pile them up in his own room.

As he carted the things into his bedroom and dumped them in a heap in the corner, he explained to Zenda what had happened.

The computer said: 'Do you mean that screeching creature, "*le chien*" as we call it in French, is going to be making those hideous noises all through the night?' Zenda began to give an exact imitation of the peke's yapping.

'Stop, Zenda, stop!' cried Tom. 'Henry's bad enough, without you doing it too.'

The machine stopped. Tom heard puzzled voices downstairs.

'What is Henry doing upstairs?'

'He's not upstairs, he's here.'

'I could have sworn I heard. . .'

Tom said to Zenda: 'You'll get me into trouble. They'll think it's me doing imitations of Henry.'

'You could never catch the sound so exactly!' said the machine scornfully.

'Well, I'm certainly not going to try.'

'Pity – it would have been fun to have a yapping contest.'

'One yapper's more than enough in this house. I hope they won't be staying too long.'

'I hope they won't be staying too long!' Tom's father used exactly the same words as they sat at their meal. He went on: 'I can't stand that woman. I really don't know why you went and agreed to it.'

'What else could I do?' said Tom's mother. 'Mum was at her wits' end. Aunt Gertrude whingeing about the damp, the dog whimpering. . .'

'Why doesn't she go back home again?'

'She's only just arrived. Mum knows we don't get on with her, but she couldn't think what else to do. She'll only be here at nights – we'll hardly see her. I'll take her her breakfast in her room – then we'll seem to be pampering her, and it will keep her out of the way.'

'Very crafty – but I don't see why you should slave like that.'

Tom's mother smiled and said: 'All right, if you insist, we'll take it in turns.'

Tom expected his father to make some excuse, but in fact he thought for a moment or two, then nodded and said: 'That's fair enough.'

'Oh, I wish you'd seen Panther. He looked at that peke as though it was some loathsome little insect.'

'It's got taste, that cat!' said Tom's father. They all laughed, except for Marion. She was sitting there glumly, pushing her food around the plate.

'Cheer up, Marion love,' said Mr Martin sympathetically. 'Aunt Gertrude won't be here for ever.'

'I don't care if she's here or not,' said Marion. There was a pause.

Then Tom's mother said, to try and lighten the gloomy mood: 'Well, I'm sure Panther cares. He didn't take to Henry at all.'

'Will Henry sleep upstairs?' Tom asked.

'I suppose he'll have to,' said Tom's mother. 'If we put him anywhere else, he'd probably yap the place down.'

'I hope he's house-trained,' said Tom's father. 'If I find myself having to step over puddles on my way through the house, then there really will be trouble.'

The phone rang. At once, Marion leaped out of her chair and rushed into the hall. Tom saw his mother and father exchange glances. Cameron was obviously on Marion's mind, as usual. Perhaps this phone call would calm her down. But it wasn't Cameron.

Marion called from the hall: 'Dad – it's Gran. About collecting Aunt Gertrude.'

Tom's father sighed. 'I'm coming,' he said.

As he took the phone, Marion said: 'I'm going up to my room.'

Tom helped his mother clear the table. He heard his father say that he would bring the car over to pick up Mrs Bellamy in about three hours' time. He came back into the kitchen and asked Tom if he'd like a game of chess.

'I can't tonight, Dad, thanks,' Tom said. 'Emma and the group are coming over to rehearse.'

'Of course, I forgot,' said Mr Martin. 'I'll go and take the car out of the garage to give you some room.

I'll need it out anyway to go and collect the Hound of the Baskervilles.'

Tom grinned. 'Thanks a lot, Dad. We'll try not to make too much noise.'

'I thought noise was the whole idea!' said his father smiling.

Tom went up to his room. Zenda's screen was busy with a succession of words and sentences in French, as it learned from the phrase book Tom had put on top of the machine.

'*Bonjour*, Zenda,' said Tom.

'Actually it's *bonsoir* – good evening,' said Zenda.

'Sorry,' said Tom.

'Do you want to try some French conversation?' Zenda asked.

'I can't tonight – it's the rehearsal. Emma and the others will be here any minute.'

'Good – I can make an assessment of their music. Perhaps I can give them a few hints.'

'You want to come to the rehearsal?'

'Certainly.'

'Well, fine, of course. But no hints, please. At least, not out loud. Emma knows you talk, but we don't want to give away the secret to Max and Marie.'

'Oh, all right then,' said Zenda, rather petulantly. 'I shall maintain a discreet silence. I shall keep quiet, stay dumb, button up, seal my lips. . .'

'Thanks, Zenda. Oh, there's the door bell. I'll let them in and get set up in the garage, then come and fetch you down, in the satchel.'

Tom went downstairs and opened the front door –

but it wasn't Emma and the Clyde twins, it was Cameron.

'Hi, Tom,' he said. 'Marion in?'

'Oh – er, yes. She's upstairs in her room.'

'I'll go up – okay?'

Tom's mother came out of the kitchen.

'Evening, Mrs Martin. Okay if I go up to see Marion?'

'Hello, Cameron. Yes, of course. Are you two going out?'

'If she'll come, yes.'

'Well – you can but ask.'

'Yes. Right . . . I will. Thanks.'

Tom thought Cameron looked a bit nervous. He seemed to be hesitating on the stairs. Then he smiled and went up. The door bell rang again.

This time, it really was Emma and the twins. After the greetings, Tom led the way through the kitchen and out the door at the back which led straight into the garage. Mr Martin came in from parking the car outside the house, had a brief chat with Emma, and went into the house.

They got the instruments out of the cases, and Max set up his keyboard and plugged it in. Marie plugged in her electric guitar. Tom and Max went and brought the speakers in from the living room, where Tom's mother and father were sitting watching television.

As they went through the hall, Tom thought he heard raised voices in Marion's room upstairs. There was nothing he could do about it – and his parents had heard nothing because of the TV. The door bell rang. Dicey had arrived.

They all went through to the garage, where the musicians were just tuning up. Tom suddenly remembered Zenda.

'I won't be a minute,' he said. 'I've just got to fetch my . . . my . . . er . . . recorder.'

Emma grinned. She knew he meant Zenda. But Max said: 'Your recorder, Tom? I didn't know you could play a note.'

'No, not that kind of recorder,' said Tom. 'My tape recorder. Just in case you want to tape something and play it over.'

He went through into the hall again, and was about to go upstairs, when Cameron appeared at the top. He said: 'All right, Marion – I'm going!'

Then Marion's door slammed, and Cameron came down the stairs.

He looked at Tom and said: 'Women, Tom! We'll never understand them.' Then he opened the front door and went out into the night.

On the upper landing, Tom could hear Marion sobbing gently in her room. He was upset. He would have liked to go in and try to cheer her up, but he thought she would be even more distressed if she thought he knew she was crying. He went into his room, and picked Zenda up. The machine said: 'I have information.'

'Later, Zenda,' said Tom, thinking the machine was going to try out its French. He put it into the satchel, put his small tape recorder in with it, and went downstairs.

The rehearsal went well. Tom and Dicey were jigging around and clicking their fingers in time with the music. Once he thought he heard a muted cry of

'Go, man, go!' from the satchel which lay on the workbench. Luckily no one else seemed to notice.

Dicey fussed a bit, wondering whether he should introduce a number by saying: 'Take it, kids!' or 'Go for it, guys!'

'It doesn't matter what you say, Dicey,' said Max, 'as long as you get on with it and stop waffling.'

'No, Dicey's got a point,' said Emma. 'Maybe it would help if we had a name.'

'A name, that's a great idea,' said Marie. 'We'll need one anyway, when the recording contracts come along.'

'How about Schoolhouse Stompers?' Max suggested.

'Or Blackboard Boppers?' said Marie.

'If it's too much to do with school, they won't take it seriously,' said Dicey. 'I think it should be called something like Dicing with Death.'

'Trust you to try and get your name in there, Dicey,' Max laughed.

'I wasn't. . .' said Dicey.

Tom heard a faint bleep from the satchel. As the others went on suggesting names, he wandered casually over to the workbench and pretended to be fiddling with the tape recorder inside. He was able to peer in, and see on Zenda's screen the words: *User-Friendlies*. He typed *Thanks, Zenda*, and came back to join the group. Emma looked over at him, and Tom winked.

He let the discussion go on for a minute or so, then said: 'I think we need something modern-sounding, to show we're up-to-date. What about User-Friendlies?'

'They'll think we're a bunch of computers,' said Dicey.

'No, I think it's good,' said Emma, smiling at Tom.

'It's dead technological, all right,' said Max.

'I'd go for it,' said Marie.

'Right!' said Emma. 'The User-Friendlies it is!'

From the satchel came a tiny bleep of approval.

They went through their repertoire of numbers. The style they had developed was a mixture of rock 'n' roll and jazz, with some slow blues-style numbers too. Max was a wizard at the keyboard. His machine could add different rhythm backings electronically, to boost the sound.

After a specially hectic number, they took a break, and Max wiped his forehead with a grubby handkerchief.

'I should really have a posh silk handkerchief,' he said, 'but my dad doesn't seem to have any. I thought of borrowing a big silk scarf of Mum's, but I don't think she would have let me.'

'You can say that again!' Marie agreed.

'Can I have a go at the keyboard, Max?' Tom asked.

'Sure, help yourself.'

Tom sat down and began tinkering with the keys. He had quite a good ear for music, and could pick out a tune all right, even if he was a bit slow.

'Hey, you could be good, man,' said Max.

Tom felt himself redden with pleasure. 'Thanks,' he said. But as he continued playing, a curious sound came from somewhere in the garage. It was a plaintive yowling and screeching, like a cat.

73

The others laughed. Emma said: 'I didn't know Panther was in here.'

'Who's Panther?' asked Marie.

'The cat next door. He almost lives in Tom's house.'

Tom had stopped playing, and the feline cries had stopped too. He started again, and once more the yowling began.'

'Panther! Where are you, Panther?' said Emma.

'It came from over there,' said Dicey. 'He must be hiding behind all that pile of paint tins and stuff on the workbench.'

'I'll have a look,' said Emma. She went and peered behind the pile of tins. She could see nothing.

She looked back over her shoulder and called: 'Play it again, Tom!'

Tom started to play, and the cries started too.

'He's here, somewhere,' said Emma, looking under the bench. Then she stood up, and started to giggle. The giggle became a laugh, and the laugh a bellow, until she was holding on to the bench, almost doubled up.

Tom stopped playing, and the cries stopped as well.

They all stared at Emma. Tom said: 'What's so funny?'

Still chuckling, Emma looked at Tom and casually put her hand on the satchel. The others were still mystified, but Tom realized now where the cat sounds were coming from. Zenda had decided to make its own comment on Tom's keyboard-playing! He began to laugh too.

The rest of them looked from Tom to Emma.

'Have the pair of you gone daft, or what?' asked Dicey.

'No,' said Emma, recovering a little. 'It's just that Panther looked so funny under the bench, crouching down in the corner. He'll never come out till we've gone. We'd better just carry on.'

Tom got up from the keyboard and Max sat down and started to play a number. The other two picked up the tune and soon they were in full swing. Tom crouched down and pretended to look under the bench. His head was almost level with the satchel. He whispered: '*Very* funny, I must say!'

He peeped into the satchel and saw on the screen the words: '*Yes, wasn't it?*'

Just then, the door from the kitchen opened and his mother looked in. She said: 'That sounds . . . jolly!'

Tom winced a little – it wasn't the word any of them would like used to describe their music. But he knew his mother meant to be complimentary. She went on: 'Ten more minutes, and then you'll have to call it a day. Bill says he can drop you all at home, on his way to pick up Aunt Gertrude.'

There were murmurs of thanks from the group. Then they gaped, as Mrs Martin said: 'I'll put Panther out here for the moment – I don't want another encounter when that wretched peke appears again!'

She pushed the grey cat into the garage and closed the door. Panther stood there, blinking and yawning.

Marie said: 'If that's Panther, what's under the bench there?'

There was a pause. Tom and Emma looked at one

75

another. Then Emma said brightly: 'You two are not the only twins around, you know!'

When the others had gone, Tom went up to his room and removed Zenda from the satchel. As he put the machine in its customary place on the table at the end of his bed, Zenda said perkily: 'I enjoyed that session! It was a lot of fun.'

Tom said with a hint of sarcasm: 'I'm glad.' He added: 'Thanks for suggesting the name, anyway.'

'You're welcome,' said Zenda. 'But now, about that information I mentioned.'

Tom remembered that Zenda had wanted to say something when he was hurrying down to the rehearsal. 'Yes, what information?' he asked.

'It's what I heard, from across the landing. Cameron and Marion.'

'Tell me,' said Tom.

'You'd left the door open, so my sensors could easily pick up the words. Besides, they were both speaking rather loudly.'

'What about?'

The machine launched into a playback from memory of the conversation between Tom's sister and Cameron, imitating both their voices with complete accuracy. Marion was accusing Cameron of two-timing her with the girl he'd gone over to talk to the other night. Cameron protested she was just a friend, but Marion was convinced that all his sudden changes of plan, and his secretiveness about what he was doing, added up to only one thing: he had another girlfriend.

Cameron pleaded with her, finally saying: 'It's not

what you think. One day I'll tell you all about it – honestly, Marion.'

Marion said: 'Tell me all about it! You won't get the chance. Because I won't be seeing you again – ever!'

Again Cameron pleaded, but it was no use. Marion began shouting to him to get out, and finally Cameron left. That was when Tom had met him in the hallway.

'What is this foolish business of girlfriends, boy-friends, two-timing, quarrelling, shouting? It is a ridiculous way to go on,' said Zenda.

'I agree,' said Tom. 'But I don't want anyone to hurt poor old Marion. She's my sister, after all.'

'Loyalty is good,' said Zenda. 'Very well – if this Cameron is two-timing, double-crossing, playing fast and loose . . . then we must do something about it.'

'What?' asked Tom.

'We will arrange a Revenge!'

Tom was somewhat alarmed. Zenda now sounded as though it was prepared to embark on a Mafia-style vendetta. 'What sort of Revenge?' he asked.

'I don't know yet,' said Zenda, 'but believe me – it won't be pleasant!'

'I believe you,' said Tom nervously.

Soon afterwards, he heard voices downstairs. It must be his father coming back with Mrs Bellamy, and the Pekinese, Henry.

Sure enough, there was the sound of yapping, and then the oozy tones of Mrs Bellamy trying to soothe the dog.

He heard his mother asking Mrs Bellamy if she

would like a hot drink, but she said: 'No thank you, just a bowl of milk for Henry. He gets so thirsty in the night. Then if you'll carry the basket and the blankets upstairs, I think we'll both go to bed, shall we, woozums? Henny-Wenny's had a hard day, hasn't oo?'

He heard them coming up the stairs. Hastily, he put the French phrase book on top of Zenda so it could absorb some more knowledge overnight. Then, in case Mrs Bellamy and Henry should take it into their heads to say good-night to him, he turned out the light and fumbled for his pyjamas.

As he got into bed, he heard his father on the landing say: 'Tom's light's out – he must be asleep. We won't disturb him.'

Tom gave a sigh of relief. The last thing he wanted was a good-night lick from Henry. He began to drift into sleep and dreams of tomorrow's disco, with the User-Friendlies having a very unmusical accompaniment from a yapping Pekinese and a yowling computer.

6

'Are you sure you want to go?' Tom asked Zenda. After the machine's screeches and cat imitations last night, Tom was naturally anxious about Zenda's behaviour if he took it to the disco.

'But of course,' said Zenda. 'I have almost perfected my French, so there is little for me to do if I stay here. Besides, I might be of some assistance.' This was exactly what Tom was afraid of. What Zenda thought was 'assistance' could in fact turn into total chaos.

But he said: 'All right, I'll take you. But promise me there'll be no cat noises.'

'Would I do such a thing?' asked Zenda innocently.

Tom smiled, and put the machine into his satchel. Today he was only too ready to be off to school. Breakfast had been a gloomy affair. Mrs Bellamy had had her breakfast in bed, but had now come downstairs and was dipping bits of toast in a cup of milk and feeding them to Henry, with an accompaniment of 'ooohs' and 'aaaahs' from her, and gurgles and slurps from the dog. Tom's father hid behind his paper, holding it up in front of his face so that he wouldn't have to watch. Tom's mother seemed distracted; she was probably worrying about Marion, who had said she had a headache and wouldn't go to work that day.

Tom and Zenda had agreed that tomorrow, Saturday, they would try to track down Cameron and find out just what he was up to. Then Zenda could draw up its revenge plans.

The day seemed to pass very slowly. Tom and Dicey and the group were being allowed to skip the last lesson of the day, so that they could get the school hall ready for the disco. Harriet Hallam and Alice Hodgkins were going to help too. Harriet had made brightly coloured cut-out masks, and figures of musicians, to put on the walls, as well as the posters. Alice was making placards that said: THE USER-FRIENDLIES and DICEY THE DISCO DJ.

As they began setting the gear up on the stage, Mr Roland appeared. The art teacher had been detailed by Mrs Forrester to 'just keep an eye on' the disco. The head had told them there would be the minimum of supervision: Mr Roland would just be around, in his Art Room, in case there were any problems – and he might look in from time to time. Otherwise it was all their own show, to run as they wished.

'Everything okay?' asked Mr Roland, brightly.

'Yes, thank you, sir,' said Tom.

'Groovy!' said a voice from the satchel slung over Tom's shoulder.

Zenda had spoken in Tom's voice, so of course Mr Roland thought it was Tom speaking. He beamed and said: 'Groovy, eh? Ah, yes, real groovy, man!'

He clicked his fingers and did a sort of hip wiggle. Tom gazed at him in amazement. He was even more amazed when Mr Roland said: 'Miss Allen and I will look in now and then, to see everything's hunky-dory.

You never know, we might take a twirl on the floor ourselves!'

That's all we need, thought Tom. Why did adults feel they had to muscle in on things? Perhaps they led such dull lives themselves that they had to wait pathetically till someone else laid on some entertainment – then they would try to get in on the act. Tom was surprised that Miss Allen seemed to be back in the picture. There had been great hostility to Mr Roland from both Miss Allen and Miss Macdonald when they discovered he had been taking each of them out, without telling the other. Tom knew Miss Macdonald was still very cool to Mr Roland – which could make for some fireworks on the Boulogne trip. Now it looked as though Miss Allen and Mr Roland were friends again.

Mr Roland surveyed the scene from the stage, then said: 'Well – see you later, alligator!'

As the teacher walked away, Tom heard a muffled voice from the satchel pipe up: 'In a while, crocodile!'

When they heard the bell go for the end of classes, Tom looked around the hall. He was pleased. They had transformed it into a scene with real atmosphere, he thought. The coloured lights, the posters and masks, Dicey and the group up on stage, rhythmic disco music already playing . . . they all made the familiar surroundings into quite a different kind of place – somewhere that promised entertainment and excitement and fun.

From his post at the door, where he was going to collect the entrance money, Tom looked up the hall towards the stage. Emma caught his eye and grinned, waving her trumpet in the air. Tom gave the

81

thumbs-up sign, smiling back. Then he was surprised to see, behind Emma, the curtains at the back of the stage open. Mr Roland's head poked out. He beamed around the stage, and said something to the startled members of the group, who nodded back at him. Then he retreated behind the curtains again.

Tom remembered that there was a way into the hall from the back, through a corridor that led to the staff room. The teachers always came in that way for the morning assembly, but the pupils weren't allowed to use it. Tom hoped Mr Roland's checking routine wouldn't be too frequent.

There was a hammering on the doors. Javed, who was helping Tom at the entrance, looked across at him.

'Okay to let them in?' he asked.

'I reckon so,' said Tom.

Javed drew aside the bolt on the door. Outside, a jostling crowd was waiting impatiently. There were cries of 'About time!' and 'What kept you?' as people surged forward. The disco was clearly going to be a great success.

Soon, the hall was full of people jigging around to the music, in pairs or on their own. Linda Morrison and Simon Viney were doing a good trade selling fizzy drinks and crisps from a stall at the side of the hall.

The music stopped. Emma blew a fanfare on her trumpet. Then Dicey said into his microphone, in what he thought were smooth, DJ-style tones: 'Hello and welcome, all you fans and ravers, to Dicey's Dare-Devil Disco!'

There was some laughter and cheering and

applause and one or two cries of 'Belt up, Dicey!' Tom thought Dicey Renton had a bit of a nerve, calling the show Dicey's Disco, when it was Tom and Emma who had thought it up.

But he warmed to Dicey again when he heard him say: 'And now, we take a break from the disco beat to hear a number live from Emma Gratton's all-star group, the User-Friendlies! Take it away, Emma!'

Emma raised the trumpet to her lips and led the way into a rousing, rhythmic number, which had the audience clapping in time to the beat. Johnny Drabble in the centre of the floor began to do a crazy, le_____ dance on his own. It looked like a cross b_____ a frantic tap dance and a Russian Cossack number. He ended with a handspring and stood there, hands outstretched, ready for the applause, which was loud and enthusiastic.

Then other people began dancing and jumping around. Tom grinned with delight. The disco was a great success. With everybody in by now, he left the entrance and wandered up the hall, the satchel over his shoulder. He had to dodge the flailing arms and jerking feet of the dancers. At the far end of the hall, he climbed the steps up on to the stage. Emma was taking a brief break while Max did a keyboard solo.

'It's going great, Emma,' Tom said. 'The group is terrific!'

'Thanks, Tom,' said Emma.

She put her trumpet to her lips again and joined in the remainder of the number. When it ended, there was huge clapping and cheering from the audience. The three members of the group bowed and smiled.

Max clasped his hands above his head in a triumphant gesture.

Then Dicey said: 'The User-Friendlies! The friendliest sound in show business! And they'll be back soon, folks, to give you more live and lively music! Right now, we've got a smooth, smoochy-coochy number from the Rozelleenas!'

He spun the disc in expertly, and a slow, dreamy number began. The dancers moved about like people in a trance.

Tom said to Emma: 'I'll just take Zenda over and leave it there behind the front curtain. Then I might go and do a bit of dancing myself.' He went over to the side of the stage. There was a chair behind the heavy draped curtain, and Tom put the satchel on to it. As he did so, he heard an urgent bleep from the machine. He knelt down, pretending to adjust the straps of the satchel, and whispered: 'What's up?'

Zenda whispered back: 'Extra voice, joining in.'

'What do you mean?'

'Listen. It is nearby.'

Tom listened, wondering what Zenda was on about. Then he heard it – a far from tuneful voice, humming and la-la-la-ing to the music. Zenda's highly tuned sensors had picked it up, though Tom could only hear it faintly. As far as he could tell, it seemed to come from behind the curtains, a few metres from the very spot where Mr Roland had looked through, earlier on. Then Tom realized who the voice belonged to. It was Mr Roland doing the hum-along with the music!

He beckoned to Emma, and she crossed the stage

to join him. 'Zenda heard something,' he said. 'Listen.'

Emma listened. Then she said: 'Who is it? And where are they?'

'I think it's Mr Roland,' said Tom. 'And I believe he's behind that curtain.'

Emma giggled. 'Let's see!' she whispered.

They tiptoed together towards the curtain. They were at the side of the stage, where the ropes that pulled the curtains were fastened to a hook on the wall. Cautiously they peeped round the side of the curtain.

In the space between the back wall and the closed curtains, a pair of dancers were turning slowly to the dreamy music, holding each other close. It was Mr Roland and Miss Allen. They both had their eyes closed, and foolish smiles on their faces, and Mr Roland was mouthing his la-la-la's.

Tom and Emma each held their hands to their mouths, stifling laughter. They drew their heads back, so they couldn't be seen by the dancers.

Emma said: 'I've got an idea!' She pointed to the curtain-ropes.

Tom grinned and said: 'Brilliant!'

They unhitched the looped rope from the hook on the wall. Slowly they began to pull on it. And slowly, the curtains drew apart. They made no sound – at least, none that could be heard above the music. When the curtains were drawn back, Tom and Emma fastened the rope to the hook, then moved quickly to the far side of the stage and down to the front, where Emma picked up her trumpet and pretended to be showing it to Tom.

Mr Roland and Miss Allen, eyes closed, continued to twirl slowly, completely unaware that they were on show. Tom heard someone on the main dance floor say: 'Hey! Look!'

Eyes turned towards the stage. There were murmurs of excitement – then laughter, which grew and swelled, till it almost drowned out the music. Soon, someone began clapping slowly, in time with the beat. Everyone else joined in.

Mr Roland and Miss Allen suddenly stopped dancing. They leaped apart from each other and stared in horror at the scene before them: a laughing, clapping audience of school-children, all gazing up at them.

Miss Allen just stood there on the stage, opening and closing her mouth like a goldfish. Mr Roland began to splutter and stammer.

'This is . . . this is . . . I never . . . who . . . ? This is an outrage!' He looked wildly around, as if he was trying to find someone to blame. But Tom and Emma and the rest of the group just stared innocently. The music came to an end, and the clapping stopped. There was a pause of total silence, when everyone seemed frozen to the spot. Then Dicey called out: 'And now, on with the music!' He quickly spun in another disc – a fast, jazzy number this time.

Mr Roland, trying to recover some dignity, rasped at the group on stage: 'Well? What are you staring at? Carry on!'

Then he turned to Miss Allen and snapped: 'Come along!' and shooed her ahead of him, off the stage.

The disco continued, and everyone was clearly enjoying it.

As Tom stood watching the dancers on the floor, he saw Joe Crabbe at the side of the hall, in a huddle with Oily Watson. He kept glancing at the stage and pointing towards Dicey. Oily was nodding and smiling agreement, in his oily way. They must be hatching some plot or other. Tom knew the warning signs.

Sure enough, when the disc finished and Dicey started to announce another number from the User-Friendlies, Joe began pushing his way through the crowd towards the stage, followed closely by his henchman. As he got near the steps leading on to the stage, he called out: 'Hold it! Hold it!'

Dicey tried to ignore him, and raised his voice: 'As I was saying, we will now get back on the all-live rhythm train with the up-to-the-minute music of the User-Friendlies!'

'I said HOLD IT!' Joe had come up on the stage now, and strode across to Dicey. Max had his hands poised above the keyboard. Emma was putting her trumpet to her mouth, and Marie had her fingers on the guitar strings. Emma was about to start playing, hoping to drown out Joe, but just then he seized the mike from Dicey, and his voice sounded out through the loudspeakers in the hall.

Joe said: 'Hello there, fans!'

'We're no fans of yours, mate!' Johnny Drabble called out. There was laughter.

Joe glared, and went on: 'I think we all agree that the User-Friendlies are a great group.'

There were cheers. Billy Morrison shouted: 'Yes, and let them get on with it!'

Joe said: 'I will, I will. But I think we all know that

what every successful group needs is a singer. And here he is! In fact, not one singer, but two!'

The musicians – and the whole audience – gazed in disbelief. Surely Joe and Oily weren't claiming they could sing?

Max and Marie looked at Emma. Dicey was trying to wrench the mike back from Joe, but Joe was keeping him at bay with one hand outstretched. Tom was about to go across the stage and tackle Joe, when Emma said: 'Let's let him carry on. The audience will soon laugh him off the stage. There'll be less aggro that way.'

'Okay,' said Tom. 'But Dicey and I will be ready, just in case.' He went across and told Dicey to let Joe have the mike.

Emma said: 'All right, Joe, sing! Let's go with 'Raving Davey!''

Joe said: 'Right!' Oily looked bewildered. Emma saw Joe whisper something in his ear. Then Emma played the introductory bars on the trumpet. Max and Marie joined in as the main melody began. Joe put the mike close to his lips and started to sing:

'Raving Davey,
Raving on the Gravy-Train,
Raving Davey,
You enslave me,
And I've got you on the brain. . .'

He held the mike towards Oily, who sang flatly:

'Woo-wah, woo-wah, woo-wah, woo!'

Joe glowered at him, and snatched the mike back. He went on singing – if you could call it singing, thought Tom. Joe's voice was rather like a rusty saw cutting into a lump of concrete; or perhaps the growl of a bloodhound with toothache.

The audience clearly had a similar low opinion of Joe's performance. They began whistling and cat-calling and shouting: 'Get off!' Joe glared defiantly and went on with the song. Oily stood droopily beside him, occasionally muttering: 'Woo-wah, woo-wah!' and looking very miserable indeed.

Dicey came towards Joe and said: 'Come on, Joe, that's enough. Give us the mike.'

Joe gave a swipe of his arm towards Dicey, who stepped back to avoid the blow. Joe was off balance. He lurched sideways, and tried to steady himself – but he tripped over the microphone cable and fell straight across Max and the keyboard. The instrument's legs buckled and it crashed to the ground, with Max spreadeagled on top of it, and Joe falling on top of him.

The audience laughed and cheered. This slapstick performance was an extra piece of entertainment. But the group on stage rushed over to Joe and Max, and picked them up. Joe shook off Tom's helping hand.

'I'm all right,' he said. 'No thanks to you, Dicey! Why did you come at me like that, you stupid berk?'

'Shut up, you moron!'

The pair of them were shaping up for a fight, but Tom held Joe back and Emma stepped between them.

'Hold it!' she said. 'Can't you see Max is hurt?'

They looked at Max. He was sitting on a chair, and Marie was kneeling beside him, feeling his arm. Max winced.

'It's his wrist,' said Marie. 'He twisted it when that great lout fell on top of him.'

'It wasn't my fault,' said Joe.

'Of course it was your fault,' said Dicey.

'Never mind whose fault it was,' said Emma. 'You ought to get that wrist looked at.'

'It's okay,' said Max. 'Look, I can move it all right. It's not broken.' But when he moved it, he winced again.

'You won't be able to play any more today,' said Marie. 'I think we'd better go home and let Mum have a look at your wrist.'

'No, you must stay and carry on with the music,' said Max.

'Don't be ridiculous, I'm coming home with you.'

'Talking of music, I'll carry on with the discs for the moment, shall I?' said Dicey.

Tom said: 'Good idea – the fans are getting restless. And I think we can do without your help this time, Joe. And yours, Oily!'

Joe hovered uncertainly, saying: 'Yes . . . well . . . it wasn't my fault.'

Tom said: 'All right, all right, it wasn't your fault – now just get off the stage, right?'

'Just so long as you realize, it wasn't . . .' said Joe.

'It wasn't your fault, yes, we heard you the first time,' said Tom. He pointed to the steps that led from the stage on to the floor of the hall. Dicey put on a record and the dancing started again.

'All right, I'm going,' said Joe.

'We're going,' said Oily, following him.

Joe turned as they went down the steps and said to Oily: 'Some singer you are!'

'I didn't know the words.'

'You didn't know the tune, either.'

'Nor did you, come to that.'

'What do you think I was singing, then, you thicko?'

They moved off down the hall, still arguing.

Tom was picking up the keyboard and trying to stand it back on its legs. But one of them was broken, and the instrument was very wobbly.

'Here, put it on this table,' said Emma, dragging a small table from the side of the stage. They put the keyboard on it and checked the plugging. Tom played a few notes. It was working.

'I'll bring it back for you later, if you like,' said Tom. 'It will save you having to carry it, what with your wrist and all.'

'Thanks, Tom,' said Max. 'You might even pick out a chord or two, while Emma plays. That would give them some live music.'

'No, it wouldn't be the same,' said Tom.

'Well, have a go, if you want to.'

'Come on, Max,' said Marie. 'We'd better get home.'

They went down the steps and moved through the hall. The dancers stopped and sympathized with Max, and thanked him for the great music. Even Joe Crabbe mumbled a hope that Max would be all right.

Dicey went on playing his records, but the atmosphere in the hall was more subdued now, and the dancing less energetic.

'I wish we could liven it up with some live music again,' said Emma.

Suddenly Tom had an idea. 'I think we can!' he said.

'I don't want to be rude,' Emma said, 'but do you feel you'd be up to it? I could show you the chords before each number, if you like, but. . .'

'You won't need to,' said Tom. 'Because I won't be playing. I'll just be sitting at the keyboard, pretending to play.'

Emma smiled with excitement. 'You mean . . . Zenda?'

'Yes. It was there at the rehearsal, so it's heard all the music.'

'Great idea! But what about . . . ?'

She nodded towards Dicey, who had his back to them, sorting out his records.

'I'll put the satchel on my lap, under the keyboard. Dicey will think I'm playing.'

Emma laughed. 'He'll be stunned to find how much you've improved in one day!'

Tom went over to the side of the stage and whispered to Zenda about the plan, which the machine welcomed with enthusiasm. Then he sat down at the keyboard with the satchel on his lap. Meanwhile, Emma had distracted Dicey's attention by going across to him and explaining that she and Tom were going to have a go at some more live music.

'But Tom can't really play,' said Dicey.

'You'd be surprised,' said Emma. 'Yesterday he was only tinkering around. He's really quite good.'

'Well, let's give it a go,' said Dicey.

When the record ended, Dicey said into the mike:

'Owing to the unfortunate incident earlier on, we are without two members of that fabulous group, the User-Friendlies. But in order to bring you some more live music, Tom Martin is going to stand in on keyboards, with Emma Gratton as usual blowing her magnificent trumpet! So . . . let's make music!'

Tom had linked Zenda into the keyboard and thus into the loudspeaker system, so that its music would be amplified. Emma played a few bars of intro-duction, to signal to Zenda which tune it was. Immediately, the amazing machine began to repro-duce the entire number, copying Max's playing, note for note, and even adding a few embellishments of its own. Tom flicked his fingers over the keyboard, giving a realistic-looking mime. Dicey stared open-mouthed. Then he voiced his admiration with the one word: 'Blimey!'

The audience gave a cheer, then a lot of them began dancing vigorously. Others came up near the stage and urged Tom and Emma on with hand-clapping in time to the beat. After the number finished, a great din of cheering and applause erupted. Tom and Emma smiled and gave nodding bows. Tom patted the satchel, then leaned his head close to the keyboard and whispered: 'Great stuff, Zenda!' There was an answering bleep.

Emma launched into another number, and the machine joined in. The dancers capered about even more energetically. Tom kept his fingers running up and down the keyboard, and turned to Emma during a pause in the trumpet-playing. They both smiled, and Emma gave a thumbs-up sign. There was no doubt that their disco had been a roaring success.

7

As they cleared up the hall after the disco, Tom and Emma and Dicey were showered with praise – everyone had clearly had a good time. Tom wished he could let Zenda have a public share of the compliments – but he would pass them on to the machine which had given such a dazzling performance.

This time, they remembered not to go off with the takings. Tom and Emma took the cash box and knocked on the door of the Art Room. Mr Roland called: 'Come in!'

The teacher was standing gazing out of the window, watching the disco fans as they straggled away down towards the school gate to go home.

'We brought the money, sir,' said Tom. 'You said you'd see it was kept safe and put in the Boulogne fund.'

'Yes, yes of course. Thank you.' He took the cash box and put it down on a desk.

There was an awkward pause. Then Emma said: 'Well, we'd better be getting home.'

As she and Tom turned to go, Mr Roland said: 'Oh, by the way. . .' His voice tailed away. Tom and Emma stopped.

Mr Roland coughed nervously, then said: 'I'm glad the er . . . event was such a success. It sounded as though you were all having a whale of a time.'

Tom said: 'Oh, we did, thank you, sir.'

'It might be better,' Mr Roland went on, in a strained voice, 'if when you're talking to Mrs Forrester or the other teachers about it, you didn't mention the . . . er . . . the little bit of dancing on the stage. . .'

'What dancing was that, sir?' asked Tom innocently.

'We don't remember any dancing, sir,' said Emma.

'Quite. Yes . . . thank you. Well, cheerio for now.'

'Cheerio, sir,' said Tom and Emma.

A voice from the satchel said: '*Au revoir!*'

The machine had spoken in Tom's voice. Mr Roland said: 'Good, I see you're practising your French.'

'Oh yes, we're really looking forward to the trip,' said Tom quickly, in case Zenda decided to launch into further French chat, to show off. Tom and Emma hurried out of the door.

They called on Max and Marie to give back the keyboard, and found that Max had his wrist strapped up.

'It's just a slight sprain,' said the twins' mother. 'He'll be fine in a few days. But no music till then, I'm afraid.'

'But look on the bright side,' said Marie. 'No writing in school, either!'

They laughed. Max said: 'How did the rest of the session go?'

'Oh, not too bad,' said Emma. 'We managed a bit of live music, but of course it wasn't the same.'

'I was just picking out the tune as best I could,'

said Tom. 'It was hopeless, compared to your playing.'

He heard a muffled growl from inside the satchel. Max looked startled. Tom rubbed his stomach, pretending he had made the noise. 'Sorry,' he said. 'It's telling me I'm hungry. It's time I was getting home.'

Tom let himself in. He could hear the television in the living room. He was about to go in, when he heard his mother's and his sister's voices, talking over the TV sound.

'But you can't be sure he's not telling the truth,' his mother was saying. 'If you had any proof, that would be different.'

'If I got definite proof, one way or the other, I could get on with my life.'

Proof, thought Tom. They must get proof, for Marion. Emma was coming round in the morning, and they were going to have a council of war – with Zenda included, of course. If there was a way of getting proof, then they could plan the Great Revenge.

Tom went in.

'Oh, hello, Tom,' said his mother. 'I'll come and get you your tea. I kept it hot. How did the disco go?'

As he ate his tea, he told his mother all about the session. He didn't mention the incident with Mr Roland and Miss Allen dancing on the stage.

'I'm delighted it all went so well,' said Mrs Martin. 'Imagine you, standing in for poor Max. Maybe you should start taking keyboard lessons.'

'Maybe I will. Where's Dad?'

'He went to a meeting they were having, about the thefts at the factory. The union says the management are hassling them too much with all the searches and so on. They want to get support for a protest.'

'Will there be a strike?'

'It hasn't come to that yet, but unless they find out how the thieving is being done, things could get a bit nasty.'

Tom resolved to consult Zenda again. There must be a way of finding out more about the situation, so that the machine could work out a possible solution.

His mother was saying: 'Dad's collecting Aunt Gertrude on his way back from the meeting. Oh, that reminds me, Tom – you know that old glass fish tank that's in the spare room? Could you fill it up with water?'

Tom wondered why. Could Aunt Gertrude be planning to give Henry a bath?

'She rang up earlier on,' his mother explained. 'She's bought a goldfish, and your grandmother hasn't got a tank. I'm afraid your great-aunt is a bit eccentric when it comes to animals. Her house is full of all kinds of strays, apparently. I just hope she doesn't start bringing a whole lot of creatures to your gran's house – let alone here!'

Tom was alarmed. He imagined the house filling up with a menagerie of strange animals. Dogs, cats, fish, parrots, hedgehogs, rabbits, gerbils. . . Aunt Gertrude was so odd, she might even turn up with a pet boa constrictor.

Meanwhile, there was the goldfish to prepare for. Tom went upstairs to fill the tank.

*

Next morning, his mother came down to the kitchen after taking Aunt Gertrude's breakfast up to her. Mrs Martin started to chuckle. Then she laughed aloud. She seemed unable to stop, and she began wiping the tears of laughter from her eyes with the tea towel.

'Come on, Mary, tell us!' said Tom's father.

Tom's mother said: 'I shouldn't laugh, I suppose, really . . . it's just that. . .' She burst out laughing again. Then she said: 'Aunt Gertrude is feeding bits of toast and marmalade to Henry – *and* to the goldfish! She even poured some tea into its tank.'

'Daft as a brush,' said Tom's father.

'But wait till you hear,' his mother went on. 'She's called it . . . Moby Dick!'

They all laughed then. Tom remembered Moby Dick – it was the name of the Great White Whale in the famous story.

'We'd better lock away the harpoons!' said his father, and they laughed again.

'I'm sorry to interrupt this mirthful scene. . .' It was the voice of Aunt Gertrude. She was standing at the open kitchen door, in the hall. They hadn't heard her come down the stairs.

'Oh, Aunt Gertrude, come in,' said Tom's mother.

'Thank you, but I wondered if I might trouble you for two more slices of toast? That fish seems to have quite an appetite. Not to mention Henry!'

Tom had a vision of a huge whale eating dainty pieces of toast and marmalade. He felt a laugh coming on, and held his hand over his mouth. He was saved by the bell.

'Oh, that'll be Emma, I expect,' he said, getting up and going into the hall, edging past the gaunt figure

98

of Aunt Gertrude, who was wearing a silky dressing gown with bright Japanese-looking flower designs, and pink fluffy slippers.

When they got into his room, Tom told Emma, and Zenda, all about the goldfish.

'At least,' said Zenda, 'it does not seem to be as noisy as the other animal.'

They began to plan their detective work to try and find proof of Cameron's deceitfulness.

'We must bug his conversation with this person,' said Zenda.

'But how?' asked Emma. 'We're not MI5 spies with microphones disguised as coffee-spoons.'

'I could do the listening,' said Zenda.

'But we can't disguise you as a coffee-spoon,' said Tom. 'Just a minute, though. Coffee – that's given me an idea. You know that café Marion goes to with Cameron – the one where he went over and talked to this other girl. Perhaps we could bug his conversation if he meets her there again.'

'How could we get near enough? If he saw you, he might be suspicious.'

'I'm sure he would.'

'But he's hardly ever seen *me*', said Emma. 'I don't suppose he'd even know who I was. I'll put on a beret or something, just in case. Then if I sit at a table near Cameron, with Zenda in the satchel, I'm sure Zenda's sensors could pick up the conversation, even if *I* can't.'

'Of course,' said Zenda.

'Great,' said Tom. 'I know what we can do. We'll

hang around in that bookshop opposite the café, and if we see them go in, Emma and Zenda can follow.'

They heard voices downstairs. Tom opened the door a crack. It was his grandmother and Aunt Gertrude, talking to his mother.

'Well, we'll be off, then,' his grandmother was saying. 'Are you sure it's all right if Gertrude stays for a while longer? It's just taking so long to get the roof repairs organized.'

'You're very welcome, Aunt Gertrude,' said Tom's mother. Tom was impressed at how sincere she managed to sound. 'I'll come out with you,' she went on. 'I need to do some shopping.' She called up the stairs: 'Bye, Tom, bye, Emma! See you for lunch. You too, Emma, if you like.'

'Thanks very much,' called Emma.

They heard the front door close. The house was empty. Tom's father was out, and Marion was working at the dress shop.

'We'll be off too, then,' said Tom.

'Can we have a peep at Moby Dick?' Emma asked.

'I don't see why not.'

They quietly opened the door of the spare room. On the windowsill was the fish tank. They went across to it. The glass was a bit green and murky from long disuse. There were bits of some kind of gunge on the bottom. Tom realized it must be the soggy pieces of toast which the fish had rejected. They peered in. The goldfish swam up and down, rather listlessly.

'Hello, Moby!' said Emma, putting the tip of her finger into the water and wiggling it about. The fish swam slowly towards it, seemed to sniff at it, and then swam away. 'All right, *be* like that!' said Emma in a mock huffy tone.

They went out of the spare room – forgetting to shut the door after them.

The bookshop was a friendly, higgledy-piggledy place, which sold second-hand as well as new books. Mr Porter, who ran it, loved books so much that you felt he was reluctant to part with them to his customers. Tom and Emma knew him well, and he was happy to let them browse among the shelves without necessarily buying anything.

Today, they hovered just inside the door, looking through a pile of books on a table by the window. They were mainly new novels, thick and heavy. Mr Porter said: 'I doubt if there's much there you'd like. Have a look over at the back, there's some new computer books just come in.'

'Thanks, Mr Porter,' said Emma, 'but we're just looking for something for my mother.'

'Oh – fine,' said the bookseller. Just then a customer came up to him with a question, so Tom and Emma were left to pretend to browse, while they peered through the window at the café opposite.

They were in luck. After about fifteen minutes, Cameron roared up on his motorbike and parked it in the laneway beside the café. Then he took off his helmet. They saw him look at another, smaller motorbike which was parked there too. He bent down and examined the controls, and put his hands on the handlebars. Then he picked up his helmet and went into the café.

Tom handed Emma the satchel, whispering into

the top of it: 'We are activating the plan. I'm handing you over to Emma.'

A whisper came back, in his own voice: 'Understood. Agent Emma is now my Control. We will infiltrate and survey the target.'

Tom was pleased that Zenda seemed to be entering into the spirit of the adventure, behaving as if it was acting in a spy saga. Tom just hoped it wouldn't get carried away. He watched Emma cross the road and go into the café. The windows were rather steamed up, but Tom could see Cameron sitting at a table. He was talking earnestly to a girl with long, fair hair. He could just see Emma, up at the counter. She took her glass of orange and sat at the table next to Cameron.

It must have been only ten minutes or so later when Cameron came out, but it seemed ages. The girl followed him. She went to the bike which Cameron had examined, and climbed on to it, putting on a blue helmet that matched the colour of the bike. Cameron said something to her. She smiled and shook her head. She started the bike and rode off down the street. Cameron climbed on to his own bike, and followed.

Tom waved goodbye to Mr Porter, who was at the far end of the shop, and went across the road, just as Emma came out of the café.

'I couldn't hear all that much because of the noise,' said Emma, 'but I'm sure Zenda got the conversation.'

There was a bleep from the satchel.

'We must hear it back, straight away,' said Tom. 'We can go into the park.'

They put the satchel into the carrier of Tom's bike and wheeled their bicycles to the small park nearby. They found a bench beside the pond where a pair of moorhens swam idly about. They held the satchel up, resting it on the back of the bench.

'Right, Zenda,' said Tom. 'Let's hear it.'

'Assignment Cameron,' said the machine in an official kind of tone. 'Conversation intercept commences.'

Then it reproduced the conversation between Cameron and the girl in the café. There were only snatches, because even Zenda had sometimes been baffled by the noise round about.

They heard Cameron's voice saying: 'Please, Jane...'

Then the girl said: 'No, I won't.'

'But you said you would.'

'I've changed my mind.'

'Oh, come on, Jane...'

There were other snatches of conversation, all with more or less the same theme: Cameron trying to persuade Jane, and Jane putting him off.

Finally, Jane said: 'I must be off.'

'I'll come along, okay?' said Cameron.

'Okay, but you won't get anywhere.' The girl laughed.

Emma said: 'That's when they got up and left.'

'Intercept terminated,' said Zenda.

Tom and Emma looked at each other.

'What do you think?' asked Tom.

'I think it sounds as if Cameron has been trying to make a pass at her – and she's playing hard to get.'

'That's what I think, too.'

There was a puzzled bleep from Zenda. Tom put the satchel on the bench and pulled the machine out a little, so that they could see the small screen. On to it came a sequence of words, as Zenda tried to find a definition:

Pass: Reaching set standard in examination. . . Permission to enter or leave. . . In football: transfer of ball to another player. . . Narrow passage through a mountain range. . .

'It's slang, Zenda,' Emma laughed. '"Make a pass" means . . . well, it means . . . wanting to kiss and cuddle and all that.'

'I see – just another pointless human activity,' said the machine.

'That's right,' said Tom, trying to avoid an argument. 'But what it means is that, thanks to you, we've got the proof which Marion was talking about. Cameron is definitely after that other girl.'

'There's only one snag,' said Emma. 'How are we going to tell her? She wouldn't be too pleased to find we'd been hanging around spying and eavesdropping, and she probably wouldn't even believe what we told her we'd heard.'

'I can reproduce the conversation again,' said Zenda.'

'But she doesn't know your powers,' said Tom. 'We'd have to say it was a tape recording or something. That's it – we'll record your interception on a cassette, and say that was how we got it.'

Emma said: 'I still don't think she's going to thank us for meddling.'

'No, neither do I,' said Tom. 'It would be different, perhaps, if the proof was the other way – that Cameron *wasn't* two timing her.'

'We shall not tell her, then,' said Zenda. 'We shall simply activate the Revenge on her behalf.'

'But what sort of Revenge?' said Tom doubtfully. He was beginning to feel they could be getting into a dangerous tangle, trying to help sort out the amorous lives of others.

'We shall devise a Revenge of spine-chilling ingenuity!' said Zenda.

As they rode home on their bikes, Tom wished the machine didn't sound quite so enthusiastic – and so bloodthirsty. . .

There was no one in when they got back to Tom's house. As they reached the landing, Emma said: 'Let's say hello to Moby Dick.' She looked in at the open door of Aunt Gertrude's room. Then she gave a cry.

'What's up?' asked Tom.

'The tank – it's all smashed!'

'Oh no!'

They both went into the room. The tank lay on its side on the floor; its metal frame was intact, but there was broken glass scattered around, and a great dark patch of water spreading out on the carpet.

'How could that have happened?' asked Tom, bending down to look at the damage.

'The door was open. It must have been the wind.'

'But the window's shut. And anyway, the tank's too heavy to be knocked over by a puff of wind.'

'Where's Moby Dick?'

'He must be here somewhere. He's probably dead by now.'

Tom put down his satchel and peered under the bed. The light was dim. He could see no goldfish, but he did see something that made him gasp with shock. Two green eyes were staring at him from the far wall at the back of the bed. There was a plaintive, mewing sound.

'It's Panther!' said Tom. 'Panther, come out of there! Panther, have you eaten Moby Dick?'

Emma said: 'He must have climbed on to the windowsill and thought he saw his lunch in the tank!'

'It's not funny!'

'I never said it was.'

'Panther, Panther, come out of there! I'm not going to hurt you. Come on, Panther.'

Tom crawled out from under the bed, and said: 'It's no good. He won't move.'

'It's too late to get Moby Dick back anyway – short of emergency surgery.'

'We can't leave him here. Aunt Gertrude would kill him.'

Suddenly, from the satchel came a barrage of barks, grunts and snarls, exactly like a fierce dog. Panther shot out from under the bed, looked round wildly in fear, then bolted through the open door and down the stairs.

The dog noises continued. Tom said: 'You can stop now, Zenda. Panther's gone.' The machine gave a bleep of satisfaction.

Emma said: 'I suppose we'd better clear up the mess.'

She knelt down and began gingerly picking up bits

106

of glass. She stood the tank frame upright, and began putting the pieces on to the hard plastic bottom of the tank. Then suddenly she shouted excitedly: 'Look! Under the wardrobe!'

Tom dropped flat on to the floor and peered. A tiny movement was visible, in the dark dusty gap under the big wardrobe.

'It's him!' Tom cried. 'He's alive!'

They both reached their arms in. Tom thought he had the goldfish in his grasp, but it slithered away.

Emma grabbed at it – then Tom again. The fish kept slipping from their grip. Finally Emma produced a handkerchief. She managed to put it over the goldfish, then tightened her grip gently around it and drew her hand out.

'He's wriggling!' she said. 'He's alive, all right.'

'I'll fill the washbasin in the bathroom.'

Emma followed him, cradling the handkerchief in her cupped hands. When the basin was nearly full, Tom turned off the tap. Emma put the bunched-up handkerchief down into the water, then took her hands out. The handkerchief slowly unfurled and floated on the surface. She picked it out. There underneath, in the water, was Moby Dick. The fish lay on the bottom of the basin.

'The shock has killed him,' said Tom.

'No, look – he's gulping.'

Indeed, the fish's mouth was moving. After a minute or so, it rose off the bottom of the basin and began to swim around.

'It's all right!'

'Thank goodness!'

They shook hands, then turned and peered into the basin at the swimming fish.

Emma said: 'He looks pretty astonished.'

'He always looks like that,' said Tom.

He fetched an old box and dustpan and brush, and they began to clear up the mess in Aunt Gertrude's room. They mopped up the damp on the carpet, and put the frame of the shattered tank back on the windowsill. It looked gaunt and derelict. Tom wondered how they could get some new glass panels for it and fill it up again before Aunt Gertrude came back tonight.

Tom took Zenda out of the satchel and put it back on the table at the end of his bed. He explained that the fish was still alive. 'I'll be back soon,' he said. 'We've just got to put the glass out in the dust-bin.'

Zenda said: 'I shall pass the time making up a poem to celebrate our great triumph over that idiotic cat.'

'You'll keep it quiet, if anyone comes home, won't you?' said Tom anxiously.

'Of course.' As Tom closed the door, the machine was reciting:

'This is the fish that lived in the tank that Tom built.
This is the cat that tried to eat
The fish that lived in the tank that Tom built.
This is the computer that frightened the cat. . .

They went through the back kitchen door into the garage, where the bins were kept. They crushed down the box with the broken glass in it, and squashed it into one of the bins.

As they came back in through the kitchen, Tom noticed some papers and plans on a corner of the kitchen workbench. He leafed through them. Then he said: 'These look like notes and drawings of the factory where Dad works. And there's a car manual too, and some diagrams. Dad must have brought them home. Maybe if we showed them to Zenda, it would get some clue about the thefts.'

They heard the car drive into the garage. Tom's father came into the kitchen.

'Hello, Tom. Hello, Emma. Those papers won't mean much to you, I'm afraid. We were all given them at the union meeting last night. They're the specifications of the current model, the factory work practices and regulations and so on – in case the management gets out of line with all this kerfuffle about the thefts.'

'Do you mind if I take them up to have a look at them, Dad?'

'I don't see why not. Are you planning a bit more detective work?'

'Well, sort of. . .'

His father was obviously amused – but he was kind enough to seem serious. 'Well, if you come up with any answers, let me know.'

'Yes, I will. Thanks, Dad.' Tom swallowed. He had to tell his father sometime about the accident with Moby Dick. It had better be now.

'Dad, there's something we ought to tell you . . .' he began. But just then, they heard a series of screams from upstairs.

109

'Good God, that sounds like Marion!' his father said. He opened the door into the hall and rushed to the stairs, calling: 'Marion, are you all right?'

Tom and Emma followed him. Marion must have come in while they were in the kitchen, without them hearing her. As they all went upstairs, Tom feared that he knew all too well what had upset his sister.

He was right. Through the open door of the bathroom, they could see Marion standing in front of the washbasin, her hands to her mouth, staring into the water. Her father went in and put his arm round her shoulder.

'What is it, love?' he said. Marion pointed to the basin.

'Good lord, it's that wretched fish!' said Tom's father. 'Don't worry, Marion. It's only Aunt Gertrude's goldfish. At least, I hope it is, and not an extra one. Or is she planning to start a fish farm? I wonder how the thing got in here.' He turned and looked with a frown at Tom and Emma, who were gazing in from the landing.

'I've told you often enough, you kids can play as many practical jokes as you like on each other, but when you start on grown-ups, they are *not* funny!'

'It wasn't a practical joke, Dad – it wasn't our fault at all,' said Tom.

'We can explain everything,' said Emma.

'Then you'd better start now!' said Mr Martin.

During the explanations, Tom got the distinct feeling that his father was trying not to smile. But even if he did find the incident amusing, it didn't stop him making Tom and Emma go out that afternoon and spend their own pocket money on a new goldfish bowl. The tank was removed and the bowl put in its place. Moby Dick had been transferred from the washbasin to a temporary home in a bucket. Tom lifted him out carefully in cupped hands.

'We should really have a launching ceremony, like for ships,' said Emma.

'Okay,' said Tom. 'You be the Queen. But make it snappy, or he'll wriggle out of my hands.'

Emma said, in a queenly voice: 'I name this fish Moby Dick!'

Tom held his hands over the bowl, opened them, and let the fish plop into the water. It began swimming round in circles, looking as astonished as ever.

Aunt Gertrude accepted the explanation that the tank had started leaking, without any question. Besides, she was more interested now in the hamster she had brought back, in a little cage with a wheel. She said it looked lonely in the pet shop. Tom wondered if it would find any improvement in having a Pekinese and a goldfish for company.

He suggested that he should bring Aunt Gertrude back a frog from Boulogne. She didn't seem to think much of this idea – and his parents reacted with horror.

Zenda said later: 'They probably thought you planned to have it for a meal. The French, I understand, like to eat frogs' legs.'

'How yukky!'

'I agree. But you are inconsistent. After all, you don't mind eating chickens' legs.'

'That's different.'

111

'Try telling the chickens that!'

Tom realized he couldn't win this argument, so he asked Zenda how its French lessons were going.

'*Très bien*,' said Zenda. 'And now I think it's time I taught *you* some. *Nous commençons demain* – we start tomorrow!'

8

So in the next two weeks before the Boulogne trip, Tom and Emma found themselves sitting like pupils in a classroom, in front of the machine in Tom's room. It used its screen like a blackboard to flash up sentences which they had to write down; and it made them repeat phrases again and again. Tom thought Zenda was a bossier teacher than most of the human ones at school.

But at the end of the fortnight, they had mastered a number of conversational phrases, to Zenda's satisfaction. They only hoped they'd have the courage to use them when they met real French people.

The lessons, and the extra time at school making maps and drawings and questionnaires for the project on Boulogne, took up all their spare time. There was no chance to activate the Cameron Revenge Plan – even if they had been able to work out what it was. Certainly, after the goldfish-in-the-washbasin incident, they didn't feel they could approach Marion on the delicate subject of Cameron's unfaithfulness. She was distinctly cool to Tom, convinced that it had been a deliberate plot to scare her.

There was a brief lull of peaceful normality when Aunt Gertrude and her creatures moved back to Tom's grandmother's house. But then the roof started leaking again because of botched workmanship, and Aunt Gertrude and her ill-assorted group moved back to spend nights at Tom's house.

It was still dark when Tom's father drove him to Emma's house, and then on to the school, on the day of the trip to Boulogne. They had a two-and-a-half-hour coach journey to get to Folkestone in time for the morning boat.

As he put Zenda into his satchel, Tom yawned loudly. He was startled when the machine mimicked the sound exactly. Then it said: 'You humans really do make some extraordinary noises!'

'I'm tired,' said Tom. 'It's so early.'

'Machines do not know tiredness – another sign of our superiority.' Tom could only agree. He was certainly not awake enough to argue.

In the kitchen, as he crammed a packet of sand-wiches and a small Thermos into the satchel with Zenda, he said: 'Don't go and eat those, will you?'

'*Très amusant!*' said the machine.

As the coach drove along and the sky got light, there was a great atmosphere of excitement beginning to build up. Johnny Drabble, who had been on a day trip to France once before, with his parents, said the French bread was long and hard, like a cudgel, but tasted good and crusty. He said he had eaten snails. Dicey asked what they were like.

'Like eating a piece of rubber – and you have to really crunch up the shells.'

As the group around him made sounds of disgust, Mr Roland leaned across and said: 'Don't mislead them, Drabble. You do not eat the shells, just the snails inside.'

Not at all put out, Johnny said: 'Is that right, sir? No wonder they tasted so foul!'

There were forty pupils in the party, and three teachers: Mr Roland, Miss Macdonald and Mr Miller. Most of Tom's friends were there – and so were less friendly characters like Joe and Oily. There had been grave doubt on Mrs Forrester's part about whether they should be allowed to go, after their behaviour during the quiz and the chaos they had caused at the disco. But Johnny Drabble said they had helped towards the fund-raising, because the money bet on Joe's doughnut race had gone into the Boulogne fund. So Mrs Forrester relented.

Tom was feeling hungry. He decided to eat a sandwich. He reached into the satchel and took out the packet and the Thermos flask. There was a bleep from Zenda. Tom opened up the small screen peering into the satchel. On to the screen came the words: *Time for another French lesson, mon ami.*

Tom typed in reply: *Not just now. I am eating.*

The machine's only comment on the screen was: *Again?!*

Tom smiled and folded down the screen and closed the satchel. He munched the ham and cheese sandwich gladly, and sipped tea from the cup lid of the flask.

Dicey Renton leaned across to him and said: 'You haven't got a spare sandwich, have you, Tom?'

Tom said: 'I'm saving them for the boat. Anyway, you had a big packet of your own.'

'I ate them when we got on the coach. I was starving.'

115

'What else is new?' Tom asked, laughing.

'You can have a crisp, if you like,' said Emma, offering her open packet.

'Thanks a lot,' said Dicey, reaching in and taking a large fistful. He began munching them noisily.

They reached Folkestone, and the coach made its way through the town towards the harbour.

'Attention please, everyone!' Mr Roland's voice came through the coach's loudspeaker system.

'Can't hear, sir – Dicey's jaws are making too much noise!' said Johnny Drabble.

'Shut up,' said Dicey, through a mouthful of crisps.

'I said, "Attention please, everyone!" ' Mr Roland repeated. He went on: 'That includes you, Crabbe. WAKE UP!'

Joe woke with a start, crying: 'What? What's up?' He stood up suddenly, banging his head on the luggage rack, then he sat down again, rubbing his head and muttering curses.

'Any more of that sort of language, Crabbe,' said Mr Roland sternly, 'and we shall leave you on the quayside.'

'Best place for him, sir!' said Linda Morrison. Joe turned and glared at her.

'Now, when we disembark from the coach,' said Mr Roland, 'Miss Macdonald will hand you each your Visitor's Day Pass. Mind you don't lose it – it is in effect your passport, and without it you will not be allowed into France. Miss Macdonald will also give you each a voucher which will entitle you to buy some food and drink for lunch on the boat.'

'Lunch?' whispered Dicey in alarm. 'What about breakfast?'

'You ate that two hours ago,' said Tom.

Mr Roland said: 'When we get on the boat, I want you to stay in a group and follow me to one of the lounges, where we shall install ourselves. Once there, you will be allowed to move around the boat, but I want no running, no shouting, and no skylarking. Is that clear?'

There was a ragged chorus of: 'Yes, Mr Roland!'

'When we arrive in Boulogne,' the teacher continued, 'you will return to base in the lounge, and we shall proceed in an orderly manner through French customs and on to our specially hired coach, or *voiture* as the French call it.'

Miss Macdonald leaned across and whispered to Mr Roland. Tom heard a tiny bleep from the satchel. He peered in, flicking up the screen. On to it came the words: *Wrong! The word for coach is autocar. Voiture means car.*

That was exactly what Miss Macdonald must have told Mr Roland, for he snapped back: '*Voiture*! *Autocar*! What difference does it make?'

Unfortunately, he said it with the microphone still near his mouth, so his words were relayed through the whole coach, causing a good deal of laughter.

Mr Roland glowered, and went on: 'As I said, you will board the coach and be taken on a tour of the old town of Boulogne, which, as you know from your studies, has many interesting features. Then after a little time at leisure in the town, we shall buy provisions for a picnic and adjourn to the beach. There the coach will collect us for our return to the harbour. At that stage I am sure your questionnaires and project books will be well and truly filled.'

There were some subdued groans, and some eager cries of 'Of course, sir!' Above them all was heard Tom's voice saying in French: '*Bien sûr, monsieur!*'

It was Zenda who had spoken. People turned round and stared at Tom, who grinned sheepishly.

Mr Roland said grudgingly: 'Very good, Martin. And you will find your French accent improves a lot after a day in Boulogne.'

Tom thought it sounded pretty good already. Clearly Zenda thought so too, for it gave a barely audible grunt of disapproval.

The coach pulled up at the harbour, and they all got ready to file out.

Tom had never been on a boat as big as the ferry, *Saint William*. He thought it was like a floating hotel, as they made their way in a chattering crocodile line, up the gangway and into the lobby area, where there were brightly lit window displays, an information desk, fruit machines, and signs pointing to restaurants, lounges and even a video theatre.

Mr Roland led the way, holding up a straw hat to guide them. The pupils straggled after him, with Miss Macdonald and Mr Miller bringing up the rear.

They reached a lounge area which ran down one side of the boat. It had fixed, comfortable cushioned chairs in rows, like a cinema, with an aisle down the middle and two chairs on each side.

When they were all seated, Mr Miller began counting them. Alice Hodgkins dived down under the seat after she had been counted, and popped up in a different place, so she would be counted twice. But Mopey Miller spotted her, and ticked her off.

Mr Roland said: 'Now, you can go off and have a look at the ship and watch us leaving port, but as I said, no larking about, and don't annoy the other passengers. You can leave your things on the seats here if you like – one of us will be here at all times.'

There was a scramble and a scurrying as everyone pushed and shoved to be first out on deck. Tom took his time – he didn't want his satchel to be bumped; and he certainly wasn't going to leave Zenda behind. It would no doubt want to absorb the general atmosphere.

Tom and Emma climbed up to the top deck and leaned over the rail.

Further inland from their own dock, they could see a smaller harbour, where the low tide had left a number of small boats standing at odd angles on the mud.

'It looks as if someone pulled the plug out,' said Emma.

Soon, there was a clanging as the big metal doors where the cars had gone in were closed and bolted. Half a dozen men in blue jackets with luminous green coverings stationed themselves in position on the deck. They wore hard hats, and thick rubber gloves to handle the ropes. One of them had a white skull and crossbones painted on his hat.

'Maybe he's a pirate, going to hijack the ship,' said Tom.

From his satchel came a faint voice, singing:

> 'Fifteen men on a dead man's chest,
> Yo-ho-ho, and a bottle of rum!'

'We're moving!' cried Tom and Emma together. A cheer went up from a group of the others who had joined them on deck. The ship moved parallel with the long pier that jutted out into the sea, then it swung out, past a fat stone lighthouse like a huge chess-man, on the end of the pier. People fishing from the pier waved at them, and they waved back.

Behind them, along the coast, they could see the famous line of white cliffs, stretching away. They were at sea! They felt a slight roll and sway as the ship moved out into the open water. At the stern, a whole lot of seagulls kept pace with the ship, squawking and crying.

Javed started to crumble up bits of a sandwich, and threw them up at the birds. Several times they swooped and dived, and caught the morsels in their beaks.

Dicey Renton said: 'Don't waste your sandwiches on *them*, Javed!'

Javed said: 'It's all right, Dicey, there's one for you, too!'

He flung a crumb high into the air. Dicey ran underneath it, and opened his mouth; but the piece missed and came down on the deck. Dicey looked down at it longingly, but decided against picking it up.

'I must say, the boat's tipping about a lot,' said Alice nervously. 'Do you think it's all right?'

'It's just the swell,' said Johnny. 'Usual thing in the Channel.'

Just then, the ship gave a particularly violent lurch, and they all staggered. Some of them grabbed the rail, some grabbed someone else to steady themselves.

'Wow!' said Javed. 'This is fun!'

'Yes, isn't it?' said Alice miserably.

'Are you all right?' asked Linda Morrison.

'Yes, thanks, I'm fine,' said Alice. 'Just a bit cold. I think I'll go and get my pullover.'

'Me too,' said Max Clyde.

'I'll come with you,' said his twin sister Marie.

The twins followed Alice down the stairway. The rest of them stood leaning on the rail, holding it firmly to steady themselves as the ship rolled and pitched. Once you got used to the rhythm, it wasn't too bad, thought Tom. In fact, it was quite exciting. He looked up at the tireless seagulls, still keeping pace with the ship. It seemed an exhausting thing to do, to fly this far on the off chance of some discarded food. But he supposed they were used to flying long distances anyway.

Emma was gazing up at the gulls too. 'Wouldn't it be great to have wings?' she said. 'We could nip across to France any time we liked.'

'It would be a bit cold up there. I'd rather go in a plane.'

'Or a balloon – like that French bloke in Boulogne, two hundred years ago.'

'Did he cross the Channel?'

'Tried to – but he crashed.' Emma had been reading about Boulogne enthusiastically, determined to make the project a success. It would be great if their group could win the Inter-School Competition.

'Hey – look down there!' said Tom suddenly. He pointed to the far side of the deck below them. 'That's Miss Macdonald, isn't it?'

121

'Yes, it is.'

Miss Macdonald was standing at the rail, wearing a smart blue raincoat and a green beret. Her red hair was ruffled by the wind. She was talking animatedly to a smooth-looking man in a neat fawn mac with a belt, and a blue hat perched jauntily on his head.

'Who's that with her?' asked Tom.

'I haven't a clue,' said Emma. 'But he looks sort of foreign. Maybe Miss Macdonald has a French lover she meets secretly on the boat. Perhaps she goes backwards and forwards to Boulogne all the time.'

'She certainly seems to speak French well, as far as I can tell.'

'Let's creep down and see if we can overhear.'

'If she's talking French, we wouldn't understand.'

There was a bleep from Tom's satchel. 'Of course!' Tom whispered to Emma. 'Zenda could understand.'

The rest of the group were also peering with interest at Miss Macdonald and her companion, and there was much speculation.

'He's just the French guide who's going to show us round Boulogne.'

'No – he's a white-slave trafficker who's going to kidnap her for a sultan's harem.'

'It's her brother, on the run from the police. This is the only place they can meet.'

'Well, we'll soon find out,' said Emma. 'Tom and I are going to sneak down on to that deck and see if we can hear them.'

'I'll come too!' said Javed.

'So will I!' said Dicey.

'No, no, she'd spot a whole mob of us,' said Tom.

'You lot stay up here and pretend you haven't seen them. We'll creep down and hide behind that bench.'

Reluctantly, the others agreed.

Tom and Emma went down the stairway, and lurked behind it till they saw that Miss Macdonald and the man in the mac were both looking out to sea. Then they ran across the deck. The benches were bulky, solid structures, fixed to the deck, with long seats on both sides. Tom and Emma sat down on the deck, and put the satchel just round the edge of the bench so that it was only a few metres from their eavesdropping target.

They strained their ears to listen, and above the noise of the sea and wind they could just hear snatches of the conversation. It was in French. They continued for five minutes or so, and then they heard the man say: 'Your French is very good, mademoiselle. I try to speak the English, but is not good.'

'Oh, you speak it just fine.'

'Perhaps we shall have an opportunity to practise.'

'Aye, well . . . you never know.'

Tom thought Miss Macdonald sounded a little flustered. She probably wasn't used to being chatted up by smooth Frenchmen on cross-Channel ferries.

She went on: 'Well, it has been very pleasant to talk to you, Monsieur Dupont . . .'

'*Enchanté*, mademoiselle, the pleasure is mine. But I am hoping that you will call me Marcel.'

'Well, I don't know . . .'

'And you are . . .?'

'Moira, as a matter of fact.'

'*Très joli nom.* . . .'

They continued in French. Tom peeped round the

123

corner of the bench. To his surprise, he saw the Frenchman counting out a wad of banknotes and passing thcm to Miss Macdonald. He nipped back behind the bench and whispered to Emma.

'Perhaps she's spying for France, and he's paying her off,' said Emma.

'But France is supposed to be on our side, these days.'

'You can never tell, in international intrigue,' said Emma darkly.

'Sssh! There they are!'

They shrank back against the bench. Miss Macdonald and Monsieur Dupont walked past them, then stopped at the door into the lounge at the stern of the ship. Monsieur Dupont raised his hat and gave a small bow with his head. They shook hands, and Miss Macdonald went in. Monsieur Dupont strolled away down the deck that ran along the side of the ship.

Tom grabbed the satchel and put it between them. They both bent their heads towards it.

'Well?' said Tom. 'What were they on about?'

The machine let forth a stream of words in French at rapid speed.

'We know you talk brilliant French, Zenda,' said Tom impatiently. 'But what did it all mean?'

'It was only polite conversation. She was telling him about the school trip, and he told her how much he liked England, and that he travelled to and fro a lot on business. He asked about the children, and she said they were not a bad lot on the whole, apart from Tom Martin and Emma Gratton, who were horrible. . .'

'Very funny, Zenda!' said Tom.

The machine gave an electronic chuckle. Then Emma said: 'But what about the money? Why was he handing over money to her?'

'Simply an exchange. She said she had to go to the bureau de change to change money into francs, and he said he would do it for her, at a better rate than the office would. He would be glad of the English money, as he would be coming back this evening, and he had a lot of French money.'

'So that's all it was,' said Tom.

'There must be more to it than meets the eye,' said Emma.

'Hold it for the moment, Zenda,' said Tom. 'Here come the others.'

The rest of the group had now come down from the upper deck, and gathered round Tom and Emma.

'Well, what did you hear?' asked Dicey.

'A lot of it was in French,' said Tom.

'But what about the money?' said Johnny Drabble. 'Are they in some international finance racket, do you think?'

Tom explained. Everyone was reluctant to accept such a simple explanation. They began to weave fantasies of plots and deals and undercover agents.

Then Don Matlock said: 'I'm hungry. I'm going to get something from the snack bar.'

'I'll come with you,' said Johnny.

'I'll come and watch,' said Dicey. 'I already used up my voucher.'

'We'll throw you a crumb,' said Johnny. 'But make sure you catch it this time.'

They went towards the door that led inside. Tom

125

heard Dicey saying as they went: 'Maybe Alice would let me have her voucher? She didn't seem to be feeling too well. . .'

Tom and Emma decided to find a more secluded part of the deck, so that they could try to learn more from Zenda about Miss Macdonald and her friend. They walked along the side deck, but there were a lot of people strolling about, or leaning over the rail and looking at the water churning by, far below.

They passed the door that led into one of the landings where stairs went down to the levels below. It was a spacious area, with glass doors on one side, leading into the duty-free Shop. This was full of people browsing along the shelves, buying themselves bottles of drink, or perfumes and cosmetics, or big cartons of cigarettes.

On the far side there was a row of half a dozen fruit machines. People were standing at them, putting in coins and pressing the buttons again and again while they watched the pictures on the rotating wheels whizz round and then stop. Occasionally there would be a clatter of coins into the chute, as a winning combination came up.

'Look!' whispered Emma, pointing to the machine on the far right of the row. Standing at it, with her back to them, was a familiar figure in a blue raincoat and a green beret, working the machine with intense concentration. It was Miss Macdonald.

9

'It's Miss Macdonald! At the fruit machine!' said Tom.

There was a bleep from Zenda. Tom held the satchel up so that he and Emma could listen.

Tom whispered: 'Yes, Zenda? What is it?'

Zenda whispered back: 'A machine to dispense fruit? I have not come across this before.'

'It doesn't dispense fruit. There are pictures of fruit on wheels that turn – if they stop in certain combinations, you win money.'

'How do you make them stop in the right place?'

'You don't. It's all luck.'

'What an unreliable machine!'

'Yes, they are.'

'Perhaps if you gave me the design specifications, I could devise a better system.'

'I'm sure you could, but they are meant to be like that.'

'A machine designed to be unreliable? How stupid.'

'Maybe, but people get very hooked on them. You can lose a lot of money if you're not careful.'

Emma said: 'I'm afraid that's what Miss Macdonald is doing.'

They looked across at the teacher. She was feeding coins into the machine, pushing the button, pushing it again, then again. Once or twice, the machine gave out a win. Miss Macdonald scooped up the coins, and began feeding them back into the slot.

Emma looked at Tom with alarm. 'You don't suppose that's the Boulogne fund money, do you?'

'That's what I was wondering.'

'Whether it is or not, we don't want her to lose it all.'

'We must go and distract her attention.'

Tom said: 'Zenda, you'll have to go into silent mode for a bit. We're going to talk to Miss Macdonald.'

The machine gave a grunting noise which Tom thought sounded rather huffy; but he hadn't got time just now to worry about Zenda sulking.

He and Emma went into the stairway landing area, and walked across to the fruit machine. They stood one on each side of Miss Macdonald.

'Hello, Miss,' said Emma.

'Oh, hello, Emma, hello, Tom. Enjoying the trip?'

'Yes, very much, thanks,' said Emma.

'So am I!' said Miss Macdonald, smiling. 'Do you know, I've never played one of these machines before – I've always wanted to. Aren't they fun? So colourful, with all the wee bits of fruit whirring round. It's exciting, waiting to see if they'll stop in a line.'

'You can lose a lot of money on them, though, Miss.' Tom felt as though they had switched roles, and he was the teacher warning a pupil.

'Yes, I suppose you can. But you can win some, too – just look at that! Four oranges! Yippee!' She scooped up the coins that came clattering into the tray, and began feeding them back into the machine. 'Oh, I *am* enjoying this!'

The wheels whirred round again. After another couple of coins, three melons came up, and Miss Macdonald gave another cry of delight.

'I'll buy you all ice creams with my winnings later,' she said, scooping the coins up.

'Miss – we were wondering if you'd like to come and watch out for the coast of France,' said Emma lamely.

'I will, in a minute,' said Miss Macdonald. 'I'll have just a few more goes at this, first. I seem to be on a winning streak just now!'

She fed the machine and pressed the start button with such enthusiasm, Tom was afraid she would go on feeding money into it until it had swallowed up everything she had, including the funds for the outing.

He hovered beside the teacher, uncertain what to do. Suddenly, someone came to the rescue – but this time it wasn't Zenda: it was Joe Crabbe.

The door was flung open, and Joe tumbled through it, looking wild and alarmed. He looked around, saw Miss Macdonald, and rushed over to her.

'Miss! Come quickly, Miss! It's Oily Watson – there's been an accident!'

'Oh, no!' Miss Macdonald was pale. 'What's happened?'

'Has he fallen overboard?' asked Tom eagerly. He didn't wish Oily any serious harm, but a rescue at sea would be exciting . . . and Oily always looked as if he could do with a wash.

'Not overboard, exactly . . .' said Joe.

'Where is he? Show us,' said Miss Macdonald.

'This way, Miss!' Joe rushed back through the door and on to the deck, and Miss Macdonald followed, without a backward glance at the fruit machine. Tom was relieved: the spell had been broken.

He and Emma went through the door after the teacher. Joe ran along the deck towards the stern of the ship. They could see a small crowd gathered near the railing, including some of the school party.

When they reached the group, Miss Macdonald said: 'Where's Watson? What's happened?'

Linda Morrison said: 'There he is, Miss. Stuck fast!'

They all looked. Oily was kneeling on the deck, his head between the white-painted horizontal metal bars of the railing. He was making a low, moaning sound.

'He was sitting on the deck, Miss,' Joe Crabbe explained. 'He said he felt sick. I didn't want him messing the deck up, so I told him to turn round and put his head through there. Then he could be sick in the sea. But he couldn't get his head out again.'

'He always was a bighead!' said Johnny Drabble quietly, and there was some giggling from the group.

'Quiet, all of you!' said Miss Macdonald, kneeling beside Oily. 'Now, the main thing is,' she said to him, 'don't panic. It will only make it worse. Just hold your head still, and we'll see what we can do.'

She turned his head gently to the left – then to the right. But it wouldn't come back through the bars.

'We'll need something to smear on the bars, and on your neck, to help it slide through,' said Miss Macdonald.

'What about Dicey's ice cream?' said Javed, pointing at the tub of vanilla and raspberry ice cream.

'Hang on! I've only just started it!' said Dicey.

'That might do it,' said Miss Macdonald, and Dicey handed it over reluctantly, with a glare at Javed.

Miss Macdonald scooped out some ice cream with her fingers and smeared it along the bars, then put some on Oily's neck. He winced with the cold of it. 'It won't be enough,' said the teacher, reaching in her pocket and producing some coins. 'Here – somebody go and get some more.'

Don Matlock took the coins and raced off along the deck, with Linda Morrison and Javed. They were soon back with several tubs of ice cream and other things on a plastic tray.

'We brought some jelly as well,' said Linda, 'and the woman in the café gave us some washing-up liquid.'

Miss Macdonald began smearing more ice cream on Oily. The others joined in eagerly to help, plastering his head with jelly. Linda gave several big squirts of the green-coloured washing-up liquid, to add to the mixture. She rubbed it into Oily's head. A great gooey lather began to appear. Oily's head could now hardly be seen, but he could be heard giving an occasional whimper.

'That'll do, thank you!' said Miss Macdonald – and then, as the helpers went on smearing, rubbing and squirting, she repeated, more loudly and very firmly: 'I said, *that'll do!*'

They all stopped and gazed at the lathered and

ice-creamed head of Oily. Miss Macdonald said: 'Now, take it easy, Watson. Just try to relax, turn your head to the side – that's it. Now pull back carefully, while I hold your head like this. Gently does it. . .'

The treatment seemed to have worked. Slowly, guided by Miss Macdonald, Oily's spattered head came back through the metal bars, and he sat down with a gasp on the deck.

Just then, a voice came through the ship's loud-speakers: 'Attention, please. In half an hour we shall be arriving at Boulogne. Will passengers with cars prepare to go to the car deck to be ready for disembarkation. . .'

They had all been so busy extracting Oily from the rails, they hadn't noticed the coast in the distance, which was getting nearer all the time.

'Look!' said Tom excitedly. 'It's France!'

Everyone cheered. In amongst the noise, Tom heard a small voice from the satchel say: '*Ah! Ç'est magnifique!*'

There was a bustling and a milling-about on the ship, as car passengers tried to find the right stairway down to the car deck, and other passengers made their way back to the lounges to gather up their baggage. After assembling in the lounge, the school group was led once more by Mr Roland with his straw hat raised aloft, this time up to the departure level landing.

Miss Macdonald kept looking round the group, her head bobbing up and down like a pigeon's as she counted the numbers. Mr Miller was looking rather grey in the face, and Alice and the twins and some of the others were looking a bit glum too. They would be very relieved to have their feet on firm ground again.

Finally they all trooped down the gangway. The dock workers were calling instructions and remarks to each other; Tom found it exciting to hear them speak French so matter-of-factly, just as he would speak English. But he was a bit depressed to find he couldn't understand one single word. He hadn't realized everyone would talk so quickly.

When they went through the customs area, Tom, with his heart pounding, tried out a muttered '*Bonjour, monsieur!*' on the official. He smiled and replied: '*Bonjour! Alors, vous parlez français, monsieur!*'

Tom reddened and stuttered: 'Er . . . *oui*. . . Yes, a bit. . .'

A voice from the satchel said fluently: '*Bien sûr – on nous donne des leçons magnifiques à l'école!*'

Tom reddened even more. He had to pretend he had spoken himself. The official looked very impressed. Luckily Mr Roland was waving at the line of pupils to move along, so he wasn't involved in any more conversation. In the arrivals area, he huddled beside a pillar, and knelt down, pretending to be fiddling with the satchel.

'Zenda, be careful. You'll give me away!' he whispered.

Zenda's voice whispered back, nonchalantly: 'Just coming to the rescue!'

'Well, wait for a signal from me, next time, please.'

'Wilco. Over and out!' said Zenda dismissively.

They were shepherded out of the building and on to a pavement beside an access road that led down to the docks one way, and up towards the town the other. Cars had started to come off the ship and were going up the road in ones and twos, with long gaps between. Tom saw that they were coming from a huge shed down on the dock, and realized they were having to go through the customs procedures in there, before they could start their journeys.

He realized something else. 'Look, Emma!' he said. 'They're driving on the wrong side of the road.'

'No, it's the right side.'

'I can see that – I do know right from left.'

'I mean it's the *correct* side! They drive on the right in France. In fact, everyone in Europe drives on the right, I think – apart from us, and Ireland.'

'It must be confusing when you get off the boat.'

They were watching a line of four cars following each other up the road. They stopped. One of the back cars hooted. The drivers peered out to see what the hold-up was. There was more hooting. The driver of the front car got out – from the left-hand side, where the driving wheel was.

That must mean it was a French car; and there was no doubt the driver was French. He began sounding off at the driver of the car behind, in a stream of angry-sounding French, gesturing violently with his arms. The other driver replied, also gesturing, then began to pull out, to get round the stalled front car.

The front driver went back to his own car to try to start it. Tom noticed the driver of the end car in the line. He was looking out to see what was happening. He had on a neat blue hat that looked familiar. It was Miss Macdonald's friend from the ship, Marcel Dupont.

He glanced across at the group waiting on the pavement, and recognized Miss Macdonald. He called out: '*Au revoir*, mademoiselle! See you later!'

Miss Macdonald gave a nervous smile, then a small wave, and called: '*Au revoir!*'

The car edged out and went on up the road, leaving the stalled car still revving and whining as the driver tried to get it to start.

'Who was that?' asked Mr Roland with interest.

Miss Macdonald blushed a little, and said: 'Oh – just someone I met on the boat.'

'Ah-ha!' said Mr Roland archly. 'A shipboard romance!'

'Don't be ridiculous!' Miss Macdonald hissed, aware that everyone was listening.

Mr Roland persisted. 'He did say "See you later". . .'

'He meant on the boat back. He's on a day trip, like us.'

'Really?' said Mr Roland. He clearly wondered if there was more to the relationship than that. So did Tom and Emma.

Just then, a coach drew up beside them. The driver, a large man with a big black moustache and a blue jacket, got out.

'*Bonjour*, monsieur,' said Mr Roland and Miss Macdonald together.

The driver launched into a stream of French, accompanied by many shrugs and pointings at his watch, and stared around as though looking for someone.

Mr Roland looked baffled. Miss Macdonald said to him: 'I think he's saying there should have been an official guide here to meet us, to take us on the tour of the town.'

Mr Roland said, unconvincingly: 'Yes, of course, I understood that. The point is, what are we going to do now? We can't wait here all day.'

'We'll just have to go without the guide. You and I and Mr Miller will have to do the explanations ourselves.'

'We'd better tell him.'

'Yes. Go ahead.' There was a tone of challenge in her voice.

Mr Roland began haltingly, talking very slowly and loudly as though the coach driver was some kind of idiot: '*Nous . . . sommes . . . er . . . les . . . er . . . teachers. . .*'

Miss Macdonald was smiling encouragingly, and with some satisfaction, at this hopeless performance. She clearly wasn't planning to help Mr Roland out just yet.

Suddenly, Tom heard a torrent of fluent French coming from his satchel, as Zenda decided it could take no more of this dithering and just had to step in. Hastily, Tom put a hand up to his mouth, as well as opening and shutting it, in a desperate attempt to make everyone think he was doing the talking.

In fact, they all did think that – except Emma – who knew the secret. After all, what other explanation could there be? No one would imagine there was a talking lap-top computer giving out this French chatter.

They were all staring at Tom in amazement – including the coach driver. Tom didn't know what Zenda had said, but the Frenchman was clearly impressed. He blinked, and started to reply in a somewhat calmer tone than before.

Tom was tapping the satchel, trying to signal Zenda to shut up. But before it could respond to the coach driver with another series of remarks, the situation was saved by the arrival of a small bustling woman in a green jacket and skirt. She was carefully made-up and her hair looked neat and almost sculptured, it was so well arranged. She had a badge on her lapel which said GUIDE.

As soon as the coach driver saw her, he again went into his tirade, with even more shrugging and pointing at his watch than before. The guide answered him back with equal vigour. The argument went to and fro, with the rest of the group turning their heads from one speaker to the other, as though they were at some verbal tennis match.

Eventually, Mr Roland hesitantly tried to interrupt. He said: '*Excusez-moi . . . nous . . . sommes. . .*'

The guide said: 'It is all right, I speak English.'

Mr Roland looked relieved. Tom was relieved, too: now Zenda would not need to display its language talents again.

There were complicated explanations about wrong information on times of arrival, and coaches being in the wrong place. Then, at last, they were told they could get on to the coach for the tour of Boulogne. They hurried up the steps. The coach driver was already in his seat, with the engine running.

When he saw Tom, he smiled and addressed a remark in French to him which Tom didn't understand. He smiled sheepishly and said: '*Merci beau-*

coup.' This seemed to be the right thing, because the driver gave him the thumbs-up sign as he went on down the aisle of the coach. He and Emma got a seat in the second row, leaving the front two pairs of seats empty for the teachers and the guide.

There was a newspaper on the seat, left over from some previous tour. Emma picked it up. She could read the date, anyway: the French months weren't all that different from the English words. 'It's today's,' she said. 'I wonder if we can make out any of the news.'

'The headline says something to do with BIJOUX,' said Tom. 'That's like the name of a café in town, at home.'

There was a bleep from the satchel on the seat between them. Tom looked in, and raised the screen. On it were the words: *Wrong! Bijoux Jewels, Gems.*

Emma said: 'And what's this word, VOL?'

Tom consulted Zenda again, and saw on the screen: *Vol Robbery.*

'A jewel robbery,' said Tom. 'I wonder where?'

'Ah! You read French! Bravo!' It was the voice of the guide. She was sitting in the seat in front of them, and had turned round when she heard them puzzling out the French words.

'No – well, only a few words,' said Emma. 'We were trying to work out what the headlines said.'

'You are right,' said the guide. 'It is about a jewel robbery. A big one, in a château near here. Several valuable antique brooches and rings were taken, when the owners, the Count and his wife, were away for the night. There is a big reward.'

'I think we are all ready now,' said Mr Roland

rather briskly. He was standing beside the guide, ready to sit down. Everyone else was already seated. Tom could just hear the voice of Johnny Drabble, a couple of rows back, softly humming the tune of 'Why are we waiting . . . ?'

'I was just explaining the newspaper to these two children here,' said the guide, 'while I waited for you to get your group organized.'

She looked aloofly at Mr Roland, then picked up the microphone and stood up, turning to address the coach.

'*Vous êtes bienvenues à Boulogne*. You are welcome to Boulogne. My name is Monique, and I shall be your guide on our tour of the town.' Then she said to the driver: '*Allons!*'

The coach moved off up the road, and soon crossed a bridge over the harbour. They could see fishing boats at the quayside, huddled together in a crowd. Above them, a horde of screeching gulls swooped, anxious to snap up any morsels of fish that might be available.

Monique told them that Boulogne was one of the biggest fishing ports in Europe, and landed a hundred thousand tons of fish every year.

'It's poison,' said Dicey with authority.

'Don't be so rude, Renton,' said Miss Macdonald. 'Just because you don't happen to like fish. . .'

'But I do, Miss!' said Dicey. 'I mean, that's the French word for fish.'

'Not quite right, I'm afraid,' said Monique, laughing. 'But nearly! The word is in fact *poisson*. You will be able to buy very good fish here, if you want. And

139

there are plenty of places that sell fish and chips, just like you have in England.'

There was a murmur of approval from the passengers. The coach went on through a street with a lot of shops, past a small square with a church in it, and up a hill towards the huge dome of the cathedral which they had seen towering over the town as they approached it from the sea.

They came to a massive old stone wall which they were told surrounded the whole of the old town. Then they went through a big entrance in the wall, past official-looking buildings, and stopped at the cathedral itself.

'We shall be stopping here for twenty minutes,' said Monique, 'while you look round the cathedral and the old town.'

'Don't forget your project books and question-naires!' said Mr Roland. There was a lot of pushing and shoving as everyone tried to get off the coach before everyone else. They spilled out of the coach, as Monique said: 'If you want to get a good view of the town, you can climb up on to the walls – the ramparts – and walk around them.'

'Let's do that first!' said Tom to Emma.

They found a stone stairway that led up on to the top of the huge walls, which were so thick that the flat area on top left plenty of room to walk around. There were even some gardens up there. Tom and Emma went to the edge and looked down over the town. They could see the port and the ships, and in the distance a beach with sand, and lazy waves, and people swimming.

'That's where I'd like to be!' said Tom.

'We're going there later,' said Emma. 'Mr Roland said so. Come on, we must fill in our projects.' She consulted a leaflet. 'It says here these ramparts were built seven hundred years ago, by the Count of Boulogne.'

'I wonder if that's the same count that had the jewels stolen.'

'I doubt it. He'd be more than seven hundred years old!'

'Very funny. I mean his family, of course.'

'Could be. But I think there are lots of counts in France.'

Suddenly they heard a loud crash. It came from somewhere below them. They peered down. There was a road running along, with trees between it and the wall. They could see the bonnet of a car buckled against the trunk of one of the trees.

'That's really smashed up,' said Tom. Car doors slammed and they heard two men's voices arguing and shouting. They must have just got out of the car. It didn't seem that anyone was hurt – just angry.

The men and the back part of the car were hidden by the leaves. The argument raged on. There was an urgent bleep from the computer in the satchel. Tom held it up on the wall, and said: 'What is it, Zenda? You can speak, there's no one else near. Not too loud, though.'

Zenda said: 'Dupont!'

Tom and Emma looked at each other, puzzled.

Emma said: 'I think it means a bridge.'

Zenda piped up impatiently: 'Of course it means a bridge. But it's a name too. The French person, on

141

the ship. It's his voice. My finely tuned sensors recognize its speech patterns.'

'Yes, of course,' said Tom. 'Marcel Dupont. The bloke that was talking to Miss Macdonald.'

'Yes, there he is!' Emma pointed.

The two men had come round to the front of the car, examining the damage. They were still arguing fiercely, with many gestures. Tom wished they were talking English – he felt from the tone of the conversation that he might learn a few new words.

Marcel Dupont was far from the smooth figure they had seen chatting up Miss Macdonald with French charm. His hair was tousled, mainly because he kept running his hand through it in a gesture of despair and rage.

The other man was dressed more casually than Marcel, in a black polo-neck sweater. He seemed to be trying to defend himself against verbal attack. Tom supposed that he had been driving the car.

It looked like the car Marcel had been driving when he waved goodbye to Miss Macdonald as they waited to start the coach tour.

'What are they saying, Zenda?' Tom asked quietly.

Zenda replied: 'There are some words that are not in the school French phrase book. I deduce that they are not very polite.'

'They certainly don't *sound* polite!' Emma laughed.

The computer went on: 'Marcel Dupont is angry with the other person for crashing the car. He says it is too badly damaged to be repaired in time for him to take it back to England today. The other man says he should get another car. Marcel Dupont calls him an idiot, and other things, and says he has to have this car. They keep repeating this argument.'

Emma said: 'I wonder if Miss Macdonald has seen him.'

'She's probably touring the sights.'

'Hey, we'd better do the same – otherwise we won't get any of our project books filled in.'

They made a lightning tour of the cathedral. Down in the maze of passageways in the crypt, they came across Joe Crabbe going on at Oily Watson.

'Just scratch it on the stone: OILY WATSON WAS HERE.'

'I can't. I'd be punished.'

'No one will see.'

'No, I mean *really* punished. By. . .' Oily's voice tailed away as he pointed upwards.

'That's just superstition.'

'Then why don't *you* write your name?'

'I will. After you.'

Tom and Emma were hovering in the passageway just around the corner. Joe and Oily had their backs to them, so they didn't know they were being watched.

Tom whispered to Emma, who grinned, and nodded. Then Tom whispered into the satchel.

Joe Crabbe was just saying: 'Go on, Oily! Don't be such a wimp. Here, I'll hold your wrist. . .'

As he grabbed Oily's wrist and directed the penknife he was holding towards the stone wall, a deep, hollow voice boomed from the machine.

'WATSON . . .' it said, very slowly, drawing out the word.

Tom clutched his mouth to stop himself laughing, as he saw Joe and Oily freeze as though they'd been suddenly turned to stone. There was silence for several seconds, while they listened in terror. Then the voice came again.

'WATSON ... WATSON ... WAS ... HERE ...!'

Somehow, Zenda made the words echo again and again, even more than they did already in the cavernous crypt.

Suddenly Oily dropped the penknife and cried: 'No! no! I didn't do it! Please!'

Then they both broke into a run, their footsteps clattering in the stone passageways. At first they couldn't find the way out, and Tom and Emma heard them saying: 'This way!' 'No, no, it's this way!'

Tom patted the satchel in congratulation, then went forward, picked up the penknife, closed it, and put it in his pocket. They walked towards the exit from the crypt, which Joe and Oily had just found. As they rushed up the steps, Mr Roland appeared at the top.

He put out his hands to bar their way.

'Well, well, Crabbe and Watson,' he said sarcastically, 'much as I admire your enthusiasm to see the rest of the cathedral, I have told you before ... NO RUNNING!'

'B-b-but ...' Oily stammered.

'What on earth is the matter, boy?' said Mr Roland.

'He was just cold, sir,' said Joe Crabbe, who looked as if he was shivering himself.

Tom came up behind the group. 'Oh, Oily,' he

said, holding out the penknife, 'I found this. It's yours, isn't it?'

'NO!' shrieked Oily. 'I never saw it before in my life!' Then he and Joe pushed past the teacher, and they didn't stop running till they were out of the cathedral.

10

'That pair will get themselves into deep trouble one of these days!' said Mr Roland. Then he looked at Tom and Emma, and said: 'I hope you two are more reliable.'

'I hope so, sir,' said Emma.

'Well, we'll try you out, shall we? You can come and help me buy things for the picnic, when we get back into the centre of town.'

As the coach pulled up in the small central square, the guide told them this was where a market was held twice a week.

'Look what that place is called!' said Johnny Drabble.

They looked across where he pointed, to the far side of the square. There was a big sign saying: WELSH PUB.

'That is definitely *not* part of your project!' said Miss Macdonald.

'Oh, no, Miss,' said Johnny innocently. 'I just wondered what a Welsh pub was doing in the middle of France.'

Miss Macdonald turned to the guide, who seemed somewhat bewildered herself – but she did her best.

'Ever since your King Henry the Eighth brought his Welsh soldiers here and took over the town, we have had connections with Wales,' she said. 'We even make Welsh rarebit, you know.'

'Thank you, Monique,' said Miss Macdonald. 'We have had a most enjoyable tour with you, and I am sure we would all like to thank you for all you have done.'

Miss Macdonald held her hands out, and began to applaud. Everyone joined in – including Zenda, who gave out shouts of 'bravo!' and '*magnifique*!' Tom had to pretend he had done the shouting, as people turned round and looked at him. He tapped the satchel in a vain attempt to get Zenda to keep quiet. He hated to be thought a show-off – but unfortunately Zenda didn't mind in the least.

Monique was smiling and nodding her head, acknowledging the applause. When it stopped, she said: '*Merci beaucoup. Vous êtes des enfants tout à fait charmants*!' Then she turned to shake hands with the teachers before leaving. As she was doing so, Tom heard a bleep from the satchel. He looked in and flipped up the screen. On it he saw the words: *Translation: she says you are all absolutely delightful children. Little does she know . . . !*

Then the machine gave a tiny chuckle.

Tom closed the screen and the satchel. Zenda's sense of humour could sometimes be a bit trying.

With a wave, the guide got off the coach. Mr Roland said they would now have an hour in which to wander round the town on their own, and after that they must be back here promptly so that the coach could take them all down to the beach for a picnic and a swim. He called for two more helpers to join Tom and Emma in the picnic-buying expedition. Dicey's hand was the first to go up, then Linda Morrison's.

When they all got off the coach, Miss Macdonald said: 'Perhaps you'd like me to come with you, to help with the ordering and so forth.'

Mr Roland took this as a personal jibe at his French, and replied: 'That won't be necessary, thank you. Why don't you stay here and have a cup of coffee, and guard the belongings if anyone wants to leave them?'

'Certainly!' Miss Macdonald sat down at a table on the pavement, just outside a café. 'Your bags can go on this chair beside me,' she said. Emma put down the bag she had slung on her shoulder, and Dicey and Linda put their bags down too. Miss Macdonald looked at Tom. He decided that for once he would leave Zenda behind: at least the machine wouldn't then have the chance of embarrassing him by ordering things in fluent French and making Mr Roland think Tom was trying to score off him.

He said: 'Thanks, Miss – I'll just leave the satchel here *quietly*.' He emphasized the word, as a way of telling Zenda not to start chattering.

Miss Macdonald looked at him oddly, and said: 'All right, Tom – I'll try not to be *too* rowdy!'

Tom gave an embarrassed grin, and the four of them followed Mr Roland, who was leading the way as usual with his straw hat held up in his hand.

Three-quarters of an hour later they came back, laden with bags containing long French loaves, butter, spreads called pâté, slices of ham, apples and pears and peaches and several different kinds of rather smelly cheeses. There were several big bottles of soft drinks too. The bulging plastic bags weighed down their arms as they came back into the square.

To their surprise, Miss Macdonald was no longer at the café table. Mr Miller was there instead.

As they dumped the bags on the ground near the table, he explained that he had been looking round the church, and had come out into the square to see Miss Macdonald sitting at the table with a man in a blue hat. When she saw him she had waved to him to come over and introduced the man as Monsieur Dupont, who wanted to show her the famous cheese shop which sold two hundred different kinds of cheese.

'She asked me if I'd mind looking after your bags, and said she would join us at the beach,' Mr Miller finished.

Mr Roland grunted, and sat down. He thanked the four of them for helping, and said they still had a quarter of an hour before the coach came, if they wanted to wander round. He fished in his pocket and brought out some coins, which he distributed amongst them.

Linda said: 'I must go and get some perfume. My mother gave me some money specially to get it for her.'

'I want to do some shopping too,' said Dicey.

As Dicey and Linda went off, Tom and Emma crossed the square, Tom carrying his satchel. They stood round the corner of the church, against the wall.

Tom looked around, and then said: 'It's all clear now, Zenda.'

Zenda said: 'Interesting encounters while you were gone.'

'So Mopey told us,' said Tom.

149

'His report was not strictly accurate,' said the machine. 'Marcel did not suggest going to the cheese shop, as she told Mr Miller.'

'Then where did he want to take her?'

'To the casino.'

'The casino!' exclaimed Tom and Emma together.

'Yes. It is a place devoted to gambling of various kinds.'

'I know,' said Tom.

'Perhaps we should go too,' said Zenda brightly. 'I have studied the theory of this game they call roulette. I have a betting system I would like to try out.'

'Not on your life,' said Tom. 'For a start, they wouldn't let us in. And besides, we haven't got enough money to gamble with.'

'Perhaps we could tell my system to Miss Macdonald.'

'I think she is probably following Monsieur Dupont's system, whatever that is,' said Tom.

'I hope he's not a con man,' said Emma. 'Perhaps he works for the casino as a sort of decoy, to get people to come in and lose all their money.'

'She certainly seems to like to gamble,' said Tom, thinking of the fascination Miss Macdonald had shown for the fruit machine on the boat.

'I think we should try and get her out, before she loses all her money,' said Emma.

'And maybe our money too,' said Tom. 'But what can we do? We can't rush in and drag her away.'

'I could imitate a fire alarm,' Zenda suggested.

'We don't know what a French fire alarm sounds like.'

'All right – I could imitate a gun-battle.'

'I'm afraid they wouldn't be as easy to fool as Joe Crabbe,' Tom said.

'Let's go and hang round outside the casino, anyway,' said Emma. 'We might think of something, and we can follow Miss Macdonald and Mr Dupont when they come out, to make sure she comes to no harm.'

When they returned to the square, the coach was waiting and people were beginning to assemble near it.

'Look!' said Emma, laughing. She pointed across to the Welsh pub. Joe Crabbe and Oily Watson were just coming out of it, looking dejected.

Tom and Emma walked across to them.

'Did they throw you out for being drunk and disorderly?' asked Emma.

'Fat chance!' said Joe Crabbe. 'They wouldn't even serve us.'

'We might have got away with it,' said Oily, 'if you hadn't asked for a double whisky on the rocks!'

'Fancy asking for Scotch whisky in a Welsh pub!' said Tom.

'I don't know any Welsh drinks,' said Joe.

'You should have asked for a leek soup cocktail,' said Emma.

They heard Mr Roland calling them from over beside the coach.

Tom and Emma asked him if they could walk there, because Emma wanted to take some photographs of the fishing boats on the way, to put in her project book.

'It's not far, sir,' said Emma, showing him a map of the town. 'We'll easily find our way to the beach.'

Mr Roland said: 'Well, all right, since you were so helpful with the picnic-buying. But don't be too long, or there'll be no picnic left!'

When the coach drove away, Emma showed Tom the map.

'The casino's just here,' she said.

They hung around on the pavement, about twenty metres away from the entrance, pretending to study the map.

Tom felt hungry. He hoped there would be some picnic left over when they reached the beach, but he doubted it. Then he cheered up, remembering the sight of Dicey returning to the coach from what he had described as a 'shopping' trip. He had a paper bag out of which he was happily munching fish and chips. Tom and Emma could always buy some as a precaution before they went on to the beach.

They waited for ten minutes, but there was no sign of Miss Macdonald.

'Perhaps she'll stay there all day, until the boat goes,' said Tom gloomily.

'Or perhaps it was all a blind and they never went to the casino at all,' said Emma.

The computer gave a bleep, and Tom whispered: 'What is it, Zenda?'

'Perhaps she has been kidnapped,' the machine said excitedly. Tom and Emma looked at one another in alarm. What if the machine was right?

But just then Emma said: 'Keep back against the wall – I see her coming out.'

'Yes,' said Tom, 'and Marcel Dupont is with her.'

The two of them stood talking at the entrance.

Miss Macdonald looked very pleased with herself. They saw her pat her handbag once or twice as she spoke. They heard the words: '. . . it was very good of you.'

'He must have helped her win some money,' whispered Emma.

'Now they're shaking hands,' said Tom. 'Miss Macdonald is looking at her watch.'

They just heard Marcel Dupont say: '. . . see you later then, Moira – at the harbour.'

Miss Macdonald walked away down the street. At the corner she turned and waved, then set off down the road that led to the quayside and the beach.

Marcel Dupont watched her go, then walked back in the direction of the small square.

'He must be coming back to England then – in spite of his car,' said Tom.

'Maybe he's just coming to the harbour to wave her off. Do you think they've fallen in love?'

'That's just soppy.'

'Why? She was in love with Mr Roland once.'

'That wasn't proper love. Nobody could be in love with Mr Roland.'

'Well, I think it could be love this time.'

There was a curious sound from the computer in the satchel. They couldn't quite identify it, but it sounded very like a yawn.

Tom was amazed. 'Zenda! Surely you can't be feeling tired? You're a machine.'

'I was imitating human sounds. You also yawn when you are very bored!' said Zenda petulantly.

'All right, we'll go down to the beach now,' said Tom.

They had been walking along in the same direction as Marcel Dupont, a good way behind him. Now they could see him crossing the road that led down towards the sea, and going back into the little square where he had met Miss Macdonald at the café table. He sat down at the same table and looked around. Then he looked at his watch. The waiter came over and he ordered something.

Tom and Emma had reached the corner of the road to the sea and were about to turn down it, when Emma said: 'Look! There's the man in the polo-neck – the one who was with Mr Dupont, having that ferocious argument about the car.'

'He's sat down at the table. They've gone into a huddle.'

The two men were sitting with their shoulders hunched, elbows on the table, talking earnestly.

'I wonder what they're talking about,' said Tom.

There was a bleep from the machine.

'I think Zenda means it could listen for us,' said Emma.

'But we can't just hang around by the table. They'd be suspicious.'

'Let's walk past them, and hang the satchel on that railing by the wall of the café. It's near enough for Zenda to hear them. Then we can go over to the far side of the square and sit on that bench, pretending to read or something. We can see them from there – and the satchel.'

No one noticed them, or the satchel. They watched from the bench, pretending to study their guide books and maps. From the gestures of Marcel

Dupont and his companion, they seemed to be getting angry again – but not loudly this time. Instead they looked almost as if they were snarling at each other. Once or twice, Marcel Dupont tapped his fist on the table to emphasize something.

They saw him pull an envelope from his inside pocket and slide it across the table. The other man glanced inside. Then the argument seemed to get more heated still. Finally the other man stood up, snapped something at Monsieur Dupont, and strode away.

Soon afterwards, Monsieur Dupont called the waiter over, paid, and then got up and walked off in the other direction, looking grim and preoccupied.

Tom and Emma retrieved the satchel, and went to the spot by the church where they had conferred with Zenda earlier.

'Well, what have you got to tell us, Zenda?' Tom asked.

'Those two do not like each other very much,' said Zenda.

'Yes, we thought that, from looking at them,' said Emma.

'*I* could tell that, *without* looking at them,' the machine retorted. 'But as I was reporting, before that interruption: there is great hostility between them, because of the crashing of the car. And there is some dispute about how much should be paid out.'

'For the repairs, I suppose,' said Tom.

'I do not know. The other man seemed angry that he was not given enough. The man Dupont said he didn't really deserve that much, since he'd nearly wrecked the whole plan. The man said he'd offered to get another car, but Dupont said it wouldn't be any use, and he was going to find another means of transport. That was all, apart from a few more words that aren't in the dictionary.'

'Well!' said Emma, 'it does sound as though he's got more on his mind than falling in love with Miss Macdonald.'

'Why was he giving her money?'

'Her winnings in the casino, I suppose.'

'He was giving the other man money too.'

'Maybe it *is* some kind of confidence trick.'

'We'll keep an eye on them both, when we see them together at the boat,' said Tom.

'Hey! *We* should have kept an eye on the time!' said Emma. 'We'd better get down to the beach.'

The beach was wide and sandy, and there were people sitting on deck chairs, and family groups of women with young children who had spread out elaborate picnics on little low tables with tablecloths on them. One or two even had small Primus stoves which they were cooking on. Most of them had a bottle of wine on the table, and some had big smart umbrellas stuck into the sand, although the sun was only shining out now and then between the clouds that drifted across the sky.

Tom and Emma had no difficulty spotting their group. They could see Mr Miller flapping his arms around and trying to subdue a battle that was raging on the sand. It seemed to be a free-for-all, and looked like one of those mass sword-fight scenes you see in historical movies; but the 'swords' were the long crusty French loaves they had bought that day with Mr Roland.

As Tom and Emma approached, they could see Johnny Drabble in the thick of it, thrashing around with his loaf of bread and making repeated stabs at Dicey Renton, who was backing away. Finally Dicey fell over backwards, and Johnny shouted '*Vive l'Angleterre!*' as he turned to ward off an attack from Joe Crabbe.

'Stop it! Stop it!' Mr Miller was shouting.

Miss Macdonald was sitting in a deck chair, observing the scene with a smile. She clearly regarded it as harmless fun; or perhaps she was thinking of other things . . .

They could see Mr Roland in the distance, at the edge of the sea. He was wearing his straw hat, and had his trousers rolled up to just below his knees. He was gazing down at his toes as the water lapped over them, and was totally unaware of the battle raging away on the beach behind him.

The duelling was continuing, but there were fewer contestants now, because the loaves tended to break in half. But Johnny Drabble and Joe Crabbe battled on, with Oily handing Joe a new loaf whenever one broke, and Alice Hodgkins doing the same for Johnny.

Tom grabbed a loaf and joined the fight, where-upon both of the duellists turned on him. Joe Crabbe caught him a swipe on the left ear, and he realized that French bread really was crusty. Just then, a football landed amongst them, bouncing off Johnny's head. They all stopped battling and looked round.

It had come from a group of boys about thirty

metres away. One of them walked across towards them, saying something in French, which seemed to contain the word 'pardon'.

'He's saying they're sorry,' Miss Macdonald called across.

Johnny said: 'That's all right, mate!' and skilfully headed the ball over to the French boy.

'*Ah, vous êtes Anglais!*' said the French boy.

'*Oui!*' said Johnny, proud that he had understood something.

'*Alors, nous allons jouer au football?*'

'They're asking you to play,' said Miss Macdonald, just as the excited reply came from Zenda in the satchel:

'*Oui! Allons jouer! Et la victoire aux Anglais!*'

Miss Macdonald looked at Tom, impressed with his command of French. Tom grinned.

With goal posts improvised from pullovers and towels on the sand, the French played the English on the beach at Boulogne. The French side were at first inclined to scoff at the presence of girls on the English team, but after Emma had scored two goals and Linda Morrison another, they didn't scoff any more.

The game was very even, and when Mr Roland, who had come up the beach to watch, shouted: 'Five minutes more! *Cinq minutes!*' the scores were level. A minute before time, one of the French players got the ball and managed to make a long run, dodging all opposition, and just edge it past Don Matlock in goal.

The time ticked away, with the English battling fiercely and pressing around the French goal. The goalkeeper did a diving save, scrambled up and threw the ball towards one of his own players. It went high, and Emma was able to intercept, giving a great leap into the air. The ball sailed off her head and past the French goalkeeper, just as Mr Roland called: 'Time!'

'A draw! A draw!' shouted the English, jumping up and down, and congratulating Emma. Mr Roland made a halting speech, half in English and half in French, thanking both teams for an excellent game. Everyone shook hands and slapped each other on the back.

Then Mr Roland said: 'Those who want to go in for a swim – you've just time before the coach comes to take us to the harbour.'

'And meanwhile,' said Miss Macdonald, 'I should like to treat everyone, including our French friends, to an ice cream!'

There was a cheer. Tom and Emma exchanged glances and smiled, remembering the money they had seen Marcel Dupont handing to Miss Macdonald outside the casino. It was nice to see that she was spending it in a good cause.

As they waited in the departure area at the harbour, Emma and Alice Hodgkins compared their project books. Alice had more than Emma, and said laughingly that Emma must have spent too much time in the fish and chip shop.

'I was busy,' said Emma. She could hardly tell Alice that she and Tom and Zenda had spent so much time eavesdropping and following people about.

Tom was looking at a box of French chocolates he had bought to take home, and wondering if he ought

159

to just try one, to see that they were all right. He heard a bleep from Zenda, and peered into the satchel, flipping up the screen. On it he saw the word: *Dupont returns. Voice identification made.*

Tom whispered 'Thanks', and looked around the departure area. At the end of the row of seats where a lot of their school party were sitting, Miss Macdonald had stood up and was talking to Marcel Dupont. Tom saw him hand her a cardboard box, about the size of a shoe box. He was urging her to open it. Miss Macdonald pulled up the lid, and took out a model of a fishing boat. It looked like the boats they had seen in the harbour.

Miss Macdonald held it up and turned it around, exclaiming with pleasure. Then she turned to the group near her, and said: 'Look, all of you! Monsieur Dupont, whom I happened to meet on the boat coming over, was very interested in our school outing. He has kindly bought us this souvenir of Boulogne.'

She held up the boat for them all to see. There were murmurs of appreciation. She turned to Marcel Dupont and thanked him.

He raised his voice and said to the group: 'I hope this little souvenir will bring back for you the very happy memories of your visit to our country.'

There were muttered 'thank you's' from the pupils. Zenda broke into a fluent and flowery speech of thanks, and Tom reddened and had to pretend he had spoken.

'*Il parle très bien, n'est-ce pas?*' said Marcel Dupont to Miss Macdonald. But Tom thought he looked at him a bit oddly. Did he suspect a trick? Or did he remember seeing him before, hanging round the square? Marcel Dupont raised his hat to Miss Macdonald, smiled at the group and walked away to join the line of people who were just beginning to go through customs before boarding the boat.

On the ship, they settled themselves in the lounge they were in before. Miss Macdonald said that when the cafeteria opened, she would treat them all to hamburgers.

But when the ship pulled away from the dock and out towards the open sea, not more than half of the party wanted to take up her offer. The rest began to feel very queasy and sorry for themselves, as they felt the ship lurching and rolling with the swell of the sea. Some curled up on the chairs and tried to sleep. Others went out to the deck to lean over the side.

The hamburger brigade munched happily, un-affected by the movement of the ship – in fact a few of them really enjoyed it.

'It's like a roller coaster!' said Johnny Drabble gleefully.

Mr Miller looked up from the depths of the chair into which he had shrunk, glared at Johnny and turned his head back into the side of the chair, closing his eyes in misery.

Mr Roland was looking pale, and trying to smile bravely as though he was enjoying himself. But suddenly he got up, wobbled unsteadily on his feet, then said to Miss Macdonald: 'Perhaps you'd keep an eye on things for a spell, Moira. I'm just going to take a little stroll on the deck. . .'

Before she could answer, he turned and made a

161

stumbling progress towards the door that led out on deck.

Miss Macdonald said: 'Thank heavens the Macdonalds are made of sterner stuff! Our family were always good sailors. After all, it was Flora Macdonald who rowed Bonnie Prince Charlie over the sea to Skye!

She sat back and opened the cardboard box, taking out the boat and examining it with approval. Tom wondered if she would have liked to keep it herself as a personal souvenir of Marcel Dupont, instead of letting the school have it. At least, now she had been left in charge, she wouldn't be able to go up and lose her money on the fruit machines. In fact, it wouldn't even be easy to play the machines at all, without staggering around as the ship lurched.

Tom and Emma decided to go out on deck. They went to the stern of the ship, where there was a small area of deck on this level – and just a few fixed benches. They sat on one of these, enjoying the wild sight of the waves and the feel of the occasional spattering of salt spray on their faces.

There was a bleep. Tom said: 'Okay to speak, Zenda.'

Zenda said: 'Constant motion not pleasant.'

'Zenda!' said Tom. 'You are feeling seasick!'

'Nonsense!' said the machine. 'I merely comment on the lack of stillness, which is not helpful to maximum machine efficiency. It is not unlike being in the carrier of your bicycle.'

'I'm sorry, Zenda,' said Tom. 'But I've got no control over the ship.'

'Or the bicycle!' said Zenda grumpily.

Tom smiled. Then he and Emma both sat up in shock. Just behind them, a smooth voice said: 'Well, hello there!'

They had not heard Marcel Dupont come up behind them. They looked round. He was holding on to the back of the bench to steady himself, and smiling down at them. They both mumbled a greeting back at him.

There was a pause, then he said: 'May I join you?'

There wasn't much they could say. Marcel Dupont said: 'Thank you,' politely, and sat down on the bench beside Tom.

'You have enjoyed your visit to Boulogne?' he asked.

'Oh, yes, thanks – very much,' said Tom.

'It was brilliant,' said Emma.

'I believe I saw you, in the square in Boulogne?'

'Yes, we were all there,' said Emma.

'I mean, on your own. You were sitting on a bench.'

'Yes, we were looking at the map,' said Tom.

'And later you were over by the church, fiddling around with that ... *sac* ... how do you call it?'

'Satchel,' said Tom, clutching it more firmly.

Marcel Dupont paused, then smiled at them. But it was a cold smile. Suddenly, he launched into a torrent of French, ending in what sounded like a question. He looked at Tom enquiringly.

'I'm afraid, I ... I don't understand,' said Tom miserably.

'Really?' said the Frenchman. 'But just now, you were speaking beautiful French.'

'Well, it sort of . . . comes and goes,' said Tom, feeling very foolish.

'It is something to do with this, isn't it?' said Marcel Dupont, pointing at the satchel. 'May I look?'

Before Tom could stop him, he had taken the satchel and opened the flap.

'A machine!' he said. 'Some kind of . . . what do you say? taping recorder, is it? But how do you record the French in the first place?'

'It's . . . very delicate,' said Tom, trying to take the satchel back. But Monsieur Dupont held on to it.

'*Je regarde*,' he said. 'I am only looking.'

He put his hand into the satchel to take out the machine. There was a loud bleep, and he took out his hand and gave a cry of pain. Then he flapped his hand around and let out a string of violent-sounding French words.

He said in English: 'It gave me an electric shock!'

Tom had taken the satchel back and was holding it close to him.

'Sorry,' he said. 'It's got faulty wiring. . .'

There was a bleep of complaint from the machine in the satchel.

Emma said: 'I'm afraid we've got to go. They'll wonder where we are.'

'Yes. Sorry,' said Tom. They edged round the bench and ran to the door that led inside, staggering a bit as the ship lurched. Monsieur Dupont did not follow. He simply stood staring after them.

As they hurried back to the lounge, Tom whispered to the satchel: 'Zenda, you're brilliant!'

'*Merci beaucoup*!' said a tiny voice.

*

They saw no more of Marcel Dupont till they were in the customs area at Folkestone. The sea had not got any calmer, and the party that walked down the gangway looked a great deal less boisterous than when they'd boarded the ship that morning.

Miss Macdonald was by far the most spry-looking of the three teachers. She shepherded everyone into the hall, and made them sit down and wait till they could go through in a bunch. Mr Roland helped her in a limp kind of way, looking almost the same colour as his straw hat, which looked out of place in the grey drizzling weather they had come home to. Mr Miller stood glumly staring at the notice saying how much drink and cigarettes and perfume passengers were allowed to bring into the country. Since he didn't seem to have bought anything, reading the notice was a bit of a pointless activity, Tom thought.

After Miss Macdonald had finished doing yet another count to see that everyone was present, she turned to find Monsieur Dupont standing patiently at her elbow. Tom could see them chatting to each other. Then he saw Miss Macdonald open her bag and show him the box with the model ship in it.

Monsieur Dupont nodded, smiling. Then he went towards the queue for the customs inspection. Tom and Emma felt he had deliberately avoided looking at them.

'I think he's suspicious about Zenda,' said Tom.

'Even if he is, there isn't much he can do about it,' said Emma. 'Anyway, right now he seems to be much more interested in Miss Macdonald and that model boat he gave her.'

'There's something odd about that boat, I feel sure of it,' said Tom.

'Let's go and have a look.'

Miss Macdonald was happy to let them look at the boat. They turned it this way and that. It was a tourist souvenir, all right, but quite an elaborate one, with masts and sails and a rudder that turned.

They were still examining it when Miss Macdonald clapped her hands and said: 'Right! Get ready everyone! We will now proceed through the customs area!'

They all stood up and gathered their belongings together, and moved along in a slow line, with Miss Macdonald at the head, Mr Roland in the middle, and Mr Miller bringing up the rear.

In the customs area there were more notices, and several low counters where people were asked to put their luggage, ready for inspection if the customs people decided to look at it. But they often simply glanced at the duty-free bags, asked what the travellers had bought, and waved them on their way.

Tom saw Miss Macdonald, at the head of their crocodile, explaining about the day trip they had all just made. The customs official was nodding. Then she looked casually in Miss Macdonald's bag. Miss Macdonald took out the box, opened the lid and showed the official the model boat. The official waved her through. The crocodile moved up, and people who had bought things showed them to the official, who simply glanced at them and waved the group on.

Tom looked over to one of the customs counters at the other side of the area. To his surprise, he saw

Monsieur Dupont. He was in earnest conversation with a customs man, and another man in a suit. He was shrugging his shoulders a lot. Then he began showing them what was in his pockets. Once or twice, he looked anxiously over towards the school party and Miss Macdonald.

Tom said to Emma: 'It looks as if Monsieur Dupont is getting a lot of questioning.'

'He keeps looking over here,' said Emma. 'Perhaps he's afraid Miss Macdonald will have gone before they let him go.'

There was a bleep from Zenda. Tom made a shushing sound, to indicate that there were too many people around for Zenda to speak out loud. He then opened the satchel and reached in and flipped up the screen. On it he saw: *Dupont spoke of finding other means of transport. He found the boat.*

Tom leaned down and whispered: 'Yes – he travelled on the boat.'

On the screen, Zenda said: *I mean the small boat. That model. He uses that instead of the car.*

Tom whispered: 'Not for travelling!'

Zenda's screen said: *No, not for him to travel. For something else. The boat has the answer.*

Just then, Tom reached the customs official. He showed her the machine inside the satchel. She simply said: 'Oh, you're a computer wizard, are you? Just like my daughter. Those machines will take over the world one day!'

There was a bleep from the machine.

The customs official laughed and said: 'It seems to agree with me!'

Tom knew she was absolutely right.

11

Emma said quietly to Tom: 'Monsieur Dupont's gone through.'

They looked across and saw him move on to the exit from the customs area, with the two officials looking after him.

When they got through into another waiting area, they saw Marcel Dupont standing there. He went across to Miss Macdonald, and they saw him talking earnestly to her.

'We must go over and keep near Miss Macdonald,' said Tom. 'If Zenda's right, and there's something odd about that boat, we must keep an eye on it.'

They moved quickly and stood near Miss Macdonald, just as she was taking the box out of her bag. 'The batteries?' she was saying.

'Yes, I forgot to put them into the boat. Perhaps if you would let me have it for a moment, I can insert them for you. . .'

Tom looked at Emma and frowned. He leaned over and whispered to her: 'I'm sure that boat doesn't take batteries.'

Emma nodded her agreement.

Miss Macdonald took the boat out of the bag and was about to hand it to Marcel Dupont, when Tom stepped forward and said: 'I'll help you put them in!'

'That won't be necessary!' said Monsieur Dupont,

so sharply that Miss Macdonald looked at him in alarm.

Tom grabbed the boat, just as Monsieur Dupont gripped it too. They each pulled at it.

Miss Macdonald said angrily: 'Tom! Let go of it! How dare you be so rude!'

'There's something wrong with it, Miss!' said Emma, her own hand round the boat and pulling, to help Tom.

Monsieur Dupont was snarling and swearing, and wrenching at the boat. Tom and Emma were pulling the other way.

'What's up?' 'What's the matter?' Mr Roland and Mr Miller had gathered round too.

'Stop it! Stop it!' cried Miss Macdonald. But the strange tug-of-war went on. Neither side would let go. Finally Marcel Dupont gave a great heave, and the boat slipped out of Tom and Emma's grasp. But the Frenchman stumbled as he turned and tried to run off. He fell forward, spreadeagled on the ground, and the boat fell from his hand as he tried to save himself. It crashed to the ground, and broke. The two halves lay there – and around them lay scattered a gleaming brooch and several rings and earrings and other jewels.

'Look!' said Emma.

'Grab them!' Tom shouted, and they both rushed forward and knelt down to pick up the jewellery. Monsieur Dupont had scrambled to his knees and was trying to beat them away with one hand, while scrabbling to pick up the gems with the other.

'*Les bijoux*! *Les bijoux*!' he was almost sobbing.

A sudden voice came shouting from the satchel:

'*Voleur*! Thief!' It was enough to make Marcel Dupont stop momentarily in alarm.

Tom called out: 'Grab him! Grab him!'

His friends needed no more urging. They rushed in a great charge, and sprawled and dived on top of the kneeling figure.

Mr Roland was shouting: 'Stop this brawling! Stop it at once!'

Miss Macdonald was standing staring, eyes wide in horror at the scene.

Mr Miller came hurrying over, with a policeman. He shouted: 'Right! That'll do!'

Then there was the most piercing whistle anyone had ever heard. It was so shrill that everybody stopped and blinked. They thought the policeman had made the noise. But Tom knew better. It had come from the satchel he was trying to shield, as he lay under the pile of helpers who had tackled Monsieur Dupont with such enthusiasm.

When the pile had disentangled itself, the policeman knelt beside Marcel Dupont, who was lying on the floor, his neat clothes now dusty and dishevelled. The policeman held his wrist, bent back just enough so that Dupont knew it would be very painful to try to struggle.

The man in the suit whom they had seen in the customs hall stood nearby, holding the jewels that had been picked up from the floor of the lounge. Tom and Emma remembered the newspaper article they had seen that morning about the robbery at the Count's chateau. Marcel Dupont must have been planning to smuggle the jewellery across the Channel in his car.

Because of the crash, he had used the model boat instead – the 'other means of transport' which Zenda had detected. If it hadn't been for Zenda, Tom and Emma, Dupont would simply have taken the boat from Miss Macdonald, and done a runner with it. He would have got away before anyone realized what was happening – and no one was going to mount a huge search for what they thought was just a snatched toy boat.

The whole school party stood in a circle, gaping in excitement, as Marcel Dupont got to his feet, still in the grip of the policeman. The man in the suit came over to Miss Macdonald and asked her and the entire school party to wait behind. They wanted to ask them some questions. Tom realized he must be a Special Branch plain-clothes detective whose job was to check people coming through the port.

The man turned and said to Dupont: 'Come with us, please.'

As Dupont was led away, he turned and glowered at Tom and Emma, muttering something in French. Miss Macdonald turned away from Dupont, looking very upset.

To try and cheer her up, Emma said: 'You were very brave, Miss.'

'Thank you, Emma,' said the teacher sadly. 'But I wasn't brave. I was very foolish. He seemed such a pleasant person. And he kindly helped me to. . .' She stopped.

'Helped you to what, Miss?' Tom asked.

Miss Macdonald hesitated. Then she sighed and said: 'He helped me to win some money, at the casino. That was why I bought you all ice creams and hamburgers. I wanted to share my winnings round a bit. I was only betting my own money,' she added hastily. She must have thought they suspected her of getting crooked money from Marcel Dupont.

Perhaps the Special Branch man suspected the same thing. He certainly kept Miss Macdonald a long time, when they asked her to come for questioning.

At last, it was Tom and Emma's turn. A policeman led them back into the customs hall and into an office that led off it. It had a desk and a table, and several chairs, and charts and official notices on the walls. Miss Macdonald was there, sitting on a chair, and looking exhausted but relieved. She explained that it was Tom and Emma who had first been suspicious about the boat, because of the matter of the batteries. The detective asked them a lot of questions.

They answered truthfully – except that they didn't reveal just how much help Zenda had been in the whole episode. It seemed unfair on the machine, but if Zenda's secret was known, it would be taken from them and examined by scientists. They didn't want to lose their companion, who had its own personality and humour.

The detective congratulated Tom and Emma on their alertness. He said Marcel Dupont was a man they had been watching for some time, suspecting him of smuggling of various kinds, but he had always been too cunning for them – up to now. They would return the jewels to the Count, and let him know who deserved the reward that had been promised. Miss Macdonald smiled fondly at them.

Tom and Emma smiled too. They were still

smiling as they nodded off to sleep during the long, late bus journey home.

Because of all the delays and their late arrival home, they were told they could all miss the first two lessons next day, and catch up on their sleep.

But Tom didn't manage to sleep late. He was woken at seven o'clock in the morning by excited cries from Zenda.

'Yippee!' it screeched. 'Zenda zaps again! Zippity-zappity-zoo! Let's hear it for the crime-cracking computer of the century!'

Tom scrambled out of bed and leaned close to the machine, giving it a tap with his finger and whispering: 'Zenda! Be quiet! Everyone will hear you!'

'Is that any way to speak to a super-sleuth?' the machine asked. 'Have some respect!'

'We know you're a super-sleuth,' said Tom, 'and you did a great job helping to work out how Dupont was smuggling the jewels, but –'

'That was yesterday!' the machine interrupted. 'I've cracked another crime since then.'

'You can't have!' said Tom. He wondered if Zenda's success had gone to its head – or whatever part of it was equivalent to its head.

'All right,' said Zenda petulantly, 'if you don't believe me, I shan't tell you!'

Tom thought it was bad enough being woken up by Zenda's fanciful boasting – it would be even worse if the machine was going to go into a sulk.

'I believe you, I believe you!' said Tom hastily. 'Why don't you tell me about it?'

'Very well, if you insist.'

'I do. Please.'

'Well, while you were occupying your time use-lessly in this curious human sleep activity, I have been busy with logical thought. Now, Marcel Dupont was originally going to smuggle the jewels out in the car, right?'

'Right.'

'So there must have been a special hiding place in that car.'

'Yes.'

'So, if a car can be used to smuggle jewels out of a country, why couldn't a car be used to smuggle other things out of somewhere else?'

'Out of where?'

'A car factory, for example.'

'You mean, Dad's car factory?'

'Exactly. The detectives and the factory managers have been searching the *people* leaving the factory. They should search the cars themselves. My deduction is that wherever the cars go immediately they leave the factory, someone there takes the stolen components from the hiding place in the cars, and nobody is any the wiser.'

Tom said: 'And whoever steals them is working in the factory, and hides them during the assembling process?'

'Indeed. So it must be a person whose job is to see to the part of each car where the hiding place is. Find the hiding place, and you will soon find the culprit.'

'But how will they find the hiding place?'

'Take a car away from a batch that's just leaving the factory, bring it to a workshop, and strip it down into pieces again.'

'Zenda, you're brilliant!' said Tom.

174

'You finally realized,' said the machine, with a chuckle.

Tom's father was surprised to see Tom dressed and ready in the kitchen when he came down for breakfast.

'You're a funny lad, Tom,' he said, smiling. 'When you go to bed at a normal time, it's the devil's own job to get you up in the morning. Yet the one night when you go to bed several hours later than usual, you're up with the lark!'

'I had an idea, Dad. About the thefts from the factory. It all came to me because of what happened yesterday, in Boulogne. . .'

His father munched his cornflakes and listened – at first casually, out of kindness to Tom. But soon he stopped eating, put down his spoon, and gave Tom all his attention. When Tom had finished, he said: 'You're a bright boy, Tom. I really think you might have hit on something there. I'll suggest your plan to the investigators, as soon as I get to work.'

After his father left, Tom was about to go up to tell Zenda the news, when his mother said: 'I'm in a bit of a rush this morning, Tom – do you mind taking Aunt Gertrude up her breakfast tray?'

Tom had almost forgotten that his mother's aunt and her various creatures were still staying with them. He said: 'Can't Marion do it?'

'No, I can't!' said his sister sharply. 'I've got to get off to work. It'll do you good to do a few things to help in this house, for a change!'

Tom knew when it was best to shut up and be as

175

invisible as possible. His sister was in a foul mood. She didn't often speak to him so nastily. He supposed she was still brooding about Cameron and his flirtations with Jane. This certainly wasn't the time to tell her about the encounter at the café. Tom doubted if there would ever be a suitable time. They might have to be content with simply trying to pay Cameron back with the Revenge scheme Zenda kept talking about with such relish.

As his mother handed him the tray, she sighed and said: 'I do wish there was some polite way of getting Aunt Gertrude to go. She's getting on my nerves, and as for your father – I think he'll explode if he sees her around here much longer.'

He took the tray. As he reached the bottom of the stairs, his mother called out: 'Don't tread on the tortoise!'

So, he thought, there's been another addition to the little zoo accumulating upstairs. . .

When he got to his own room, he went across to the table where the computer was standing. He was about to start telling Zenda how his father had praised the plan, when he noticed a list on the screen. He read it:

1. *Punctures*
2. *Sugar in petrol tank*
3. *Loosen wheel-nuts*
4. *Disconnect brakes*

'What's this, Zenda?' asked Tom. 'More detective work about the car factory?'

176

'No,' said the machine. 'I am working on another vehicle now – Cameron's motorbike. I am listing possible ways of interfering with his bike so as to cause him problems, as a Revenge.'

'Some of those ways would cause him more than problems, they'd be absolute disaster.'

'Revenge is not meant to be pleasant.'

'We don't want it to be deadly, either.'

'We shall see,' said Zenda mysteriously.

'There's another problem I'd like you to think about,' said Tom.

To distract Zenda's attention from plotting against Cameron with increasingly dangerous schemes, Tom described how fed up his mother and father were with Aunt Gertrude and her growing menagerie of creatures.

'I will consider possible solutions,' said Zenda.

'Well, try to make them harmless, this time,' said Tom.

'As you wish,' said Zenda.

Tom thought the machine sounded disappointed.

At school, every spare moment of the day was filled with telling and retelling the events of the trip to Boulogne to those who had not been there.

The accounts got more and more fantastic as the storytellers realized what an eager audience they had. In the lunch break, the playground was scattered with small groups, each spellbound by one narrative or another.

Tom and Emma were the centre of one group. They didn't have to do any embroidering on their story – it was exciting enough already – though they had to leave out any description of Zenda's role in the events.

Occasionally, as Emma was speaking, Tom listened to snatches of tales that he could hear from the other groups.

He heard Dicey say: 'Of course, I was suspicious of the bloke from the start. . .'

Johnny Drabble was saying: 'You see, when you're as familiar with sea travel as I am, you're alert to anything suspicious. . .'

Most exaggerated of all was Joe Crabbe, whom Tom overheard boasting: '. . . and so I gave the crook a judo throw and brought him to the ground, then with a quick uppercut to the jaw I laid him out cold. . .'

Tom smiled. It was a pity Zenda couldn't be asked to tell its own story of the events of that day. No doubt its account would rival any of the others in colourfulness – and, of course, there would be no doubt whatever about who would have the starring role. . .

When Tom got home that day, Zenda announced that it had come up with a foolproof scheme to make Aunt Gertrude decide to leave of her own accord.

'You are aware, I am sure,' said the machine, 'that dogs can hear sounds way out of reach of the hearing capabilities of you humans.'

'Yes. I suppose even Henry the Pekinese can do that.'

'Precisely – and it's Henry I want to hear the sounds.'

'But who's going to make them?'

'I am. Now, here's what I want you to do. . .'

Tom laughed when he heard the plan. He hoped he would be able to keep a straight face.

That evening, his father came home very excited; he told Tom that the investigators had been very impressed with what he had suggested. They had asked him to say nothing to anyone at the factory, while they made preparations to follow the plan. The big swoop would happen when the first batch of cars came out of the factory next day.

When Tom came downstairs in the morning, his father was just getting ready to go to the factory. He was going to be with the detectives when they put the plan into action.

'I'm very grateful to you, Tom,' he said. 'Maybe you'll be a detective yourself, one day!'

Tom smiled with pleasure, thinking it was much easier to do detective work if you had the help of a super-sleuth like Zenda.

As he ate breakfast, Tom watched his mother preparing the tray for Aunt Gertrude. She and Marion looked very surprised when he offered to take it upstairs. They didn't know that this was a vital part of Zenda's Plan for Getting Rid of Aunt Gertrude.

He stepped carefully over the tortoise and put the tray down on the table beside the bed. He looked at Henry, who was curled up on the bed and had opened one big eye to look at him.

'Do you think it's true that dogs can hear things we can't?' asked Tom conversationally.

'Certainly!' said Aunt Gertrude, pouring herself some tea. 'They are much more sensitive than we are.'

'So they could even detect things we wouldn't know were there at all?'

'What sort of things?'

'Say . . . ghosts and such. Supernatural things.'

'Well, you do hear of dogs becoming agitated in haunted houses.'

'And Henry hasn't been agitated since he's been here?'

'No, of course not – have you, Henny-Wenny?' She stroked the dog's head, and it gave a slobbery kind of smile. 'What could agitate my little lovey-dovey here?'

'Oh, I just wondered. I suppose nobody mentioned anything to you about the hauntings. . .'

'Hauntings? What hauntings?'

'Oh, it was just a rumour someone told us, about this house. But of course we didn't believe it. You couldn't have a ghost of a wolfhound, anyway – it would be too big.'

'Wolfhounds? Those huge savage dogs?'

'Yes, one used to live here. And there was an accident. But as I say, nobody believes the rumours about the hauntings.'

'I should think not, indeed! Canine ghosts? What stuff and nonsense – isn't it, Henny-Wenny?' But Tom thought she looked a little worried, all the same.

Emma came to Tom's house after school, and Mrs Martin asked her to stay for the evening meal. They were up in Tom's room gazing in some puzzlement at

Zenda as it practised what it claimed was its 'Sounds Beyond Human Hearing' routine. They could hear nothing, but the machine insisted they remain silent while it tried out its sequence of sounds.

After a few minutes, Tom whispered to Emma: 'Do you think it's fooling us – just having a joke, and not really doing anything?'

'Certainly not!' came an outraged voice from the machine. 'Would *I* play a trick like that?'

Nothing was more likely, thought Tom. But he simply said: 'Sorry, Zenda.'

'You wait till tomorrow morning, then you'll know I wasn't playing any tricks – at least, not on *you*!'

Zenda's plan was for Tom to put it into his satchel and, when everyone was in bed, to put the satchel just outside Aunt Gertrude's door. No one would hear anything during the night – except Henry, the Pekinese. . .

Tom heard the roar of a motorbike coming to a stop outside.

'That must be Cameron, mustn't it?' said Emma.

'He doesn't come round any more,' said Tom. 'But I can't think who else it can be.'

They went to the top of the stairs. They saw Tom's mother go to the front door and open it. It was indeed Cameron on the doorstep.

'Hello, Mrs Martin,' said Cameron cheerfully, as if he was as welcome as ever.

'Hello, Cameron,' said Mrs Martin, rather coolly. 'Can I see Marion?'

'I . . . I'll see if she's in,' said Tom's mother. She went into the living room.

Tom knew that Marion was in, but his mother was

being tactful. She must be whispering to Marion, asking if she would rather pretend to be out.

Cameron glanced up the stairs and saw Tom and Emma standing there.

'Hello, you two,' he said amiably. 'Doing a bit of eavesdropping?'

'Oh! No, no,' said Tom. 'We were just coming down.' He was glad Cameron didn't know just how much eavesdropping they had already been doing, with Zenda's help.

They had started down the stairs when Marion came out of the living room into the hall. Her mother went through the hall into the kitchen and closed the door. Tom and Emma decided it was their turn to be tactful, and retreated up the stairs again. Tom put his fingers to his lips, then opened and closed his door, while actually remaining on the landing. That way, Marion and Cameron would think they had gone. They kept out of sight round the corner of the landing, and listened.

At first, Marion was very sharp and aloof. But Cameron kept explaining that there was nothing between him and Jane. Finally he said: 'I was seeing her, sure. But it wasn't what you think, at all. I wanted to buy something off her, as a surprise for you. That's why I couldn't tell you before.'

'What kind of surprise?' asked Marion, suspiciously.

'Come and see!'

She followed him out of the front door.

'We can see from the window of the spare room,' said Tom.

They peered out of the window. There, beside the

gate with Cameron and Marion admiring it, was a blue motorbike – the one they had seen Jane ride away on from the café.

Marion leaned towards the bike, her face full of excitement. She gripped the handlebars delightedly. Then she turned and gave Cameron a big hug.

Emma and Tom smiled at each other. 'Well, thank goodness for that,' said Tom. 'Now Marion will be a bit more cheerful around the place, and won't keep snapping my head off.'

'And we won't have to keep stalling Zenda from inventing more and more horrible Revenges!'

They went into Tom's room to tell Zenda what had happened. The machine seemed disappointed, but it was anxious to defend its deductions. It began to repeat from its memory the café conversation it had bugged:

'Please, Jane. . .'

'No, I won't.'

'But you said you would.'

'I've changed my mind.'

After playing through the conversation, Zenda said: 'The deduction was accurate enough, given the information provided.'

'Of course it was,' said Tom. 'We deduced the same thing. Well, we all make mistakes.'

'*I* don't!' said Zenda, huffily. 'I was simply given insufficient data!'

Tom and Emma decided not to argue. Just then, they heard the roar of a motorbike starting up, and Tom's mother at the door, calling: 'Take care, now!'

They went through into the spare room, in time to see the blue bike speeding off down the road, with

Marion in her painted helmet in front, and Cameron riding on the pillion.

Soon afterwards, Tom's father came home in a state of great excitement. The plan had worked. It seemed that the stolen components were being hidden underneath the spare tyre, which was strapped into its own space near the engine. Three arrests had been made. The manager had congratulated Tom's father on his astuteness, and so had the detectives. There would be a considerable extra sum in Mr Martin's next pay packet.

'I told them it all came from an idea of my son's,' said Tom's father. 'The manager said that when you're old enough there could well be a job for you in the factory. And the detectives said there could well be a job for you in Scotland Yard!'

They all laughed happily.

'Meanwhile,' said Mr Martin, 'I'm to bring you to the factory on Monday, for a special lunch and presentation.'

Tom felt very proud to have been able to help his father. And tonight, if things worked out all right, he would help him and the whole family in another way: by getting Aunt Gertrude to decide to move out.

Tom set his alarm clock, and put it under his pillow. It woke him at midnight. He got out of bed, went to the door, and opened it a little. The house was in darkness, and there was no sound. He put Zenda into the satchel, and whispered: 'Good luck!'

'Thanks, Tom!' said the machine. 'I'll do my best for you.'

'Thanks, Zenda!' said Tom. 'You always do.'

Tom put the satchel down, just beside the door and leaning against the wall. With any luck, if Aunt Gertrude went to the bathroom in the night, she wouldn't notice the satchel. Even if she did, she would just think Tom had carelessly left it there.

The alarm went again under the pillow at six o'clock in the morning. Tom crept out to retrieve the satchel, as he and Zenda had planned. This time, Tom paused to listen at Aunt Gertrude's door. He could definitely hear some whimpering coming from Henry, and the voice of Aunt Gertrude comforting him.

Back in his room, he took the machine out of the satchel and said: 'Well done, Zenda, it seems to have worked. I never heard a thing during the night, myself.'

'Ah, but Henry did!' said Zenda.

At breakfast, they were all surprised when the door opened and there stood Aunt Gertrude, fully dressed and with her outdoor coat and hat on.

She explained that she would have to leave that day. She would be going home again. She would leave the family the goldfish and the tortoise, since they would be hard to transport. She thought her sister, Tom's grandmother, was sure to like the hamster. Tom was less sure, but he said nothing.

Henry, of course, would be coming with her. 'Poor Henry,' she said. 'He is so very sensitive. I must say I have never believed in the supernatural myself, but now I am not so certain.'

185

'The supernatural? What are you talking about, Aunt Gertrude?' asked Tom's mother in amazement.

'I think you know,' said Aunt Gertrude darkly. 'You might have told me – even if it *was* only a rumour.'

'Told you what? I'm totally baffled,' said Mrs Martin.

But Aunt Gertrude simply shook her head, and said: 'Poor Henry. He was waking up constantly, and growling and whimpering. Of course, I couldn't let him suffer another night of it.'

'But Aunt Gertrude . . .' said Tom's mother.

His father interrupted: 'Now Mary, we're all very sorry of course that Aunt Gertrude won't be with us any longer, but if she feels she must get home we mustn't stand in her way.'

Tom felt that his father was just as mystified as his mother, but wasn't going to risk Aunt Gertrude changing her mind.

Mr Martin went on: 'They've given me a day off today. I can run you to the station, whenever you like.'

Tom had rarely seen his father give such a beaming smile.

On the following Monday, Tom brought Zenda to school. His father was coming to collect him and take him to the factory for the lunch and presentation; and he had persuaded Mrs Forrester to let him have the afternoon off. Tom was determined that Zenda should be with him to hear what was said at the factory – even if the machine would not be able to receive its true share of the compliments.

186

So Zenda was there at the morning assembly, to hear yet more exciting news. Mrs Forrester announced that she had just heard from the French count whose jewels they had helped to recover. He would be giving a substantial sum of money to the school, as a reward. They had not decided how to spend it yet, but it would probably go towards the fund for building a school swimming pool. There was applause.

Then Mrs Forrester went on to say: 'The Count has also asked me to pass on an invitation. He would like Tom Martin and Emma Gratton, as the people whose quick thinking really saved the jewels, to come and spend a weekend as his guests in his château near Boulogne – and to bring half a dozen of their friends with them!'

At this, there was even more applause. People leaned forward to pat Tom and Emma on the back and congratulate them. Tom heard a tiny voice from the satchel say: '*Magnifique!*'

Later, in a corner of the playground, Tom and Emma were chatting together on their own, eagerly talking about the wonderful news about their invitation to the château.

Tom leaned down to the satchel and whispered: 'Most of it is thanks to you, Zenda. You really are an amazing machine!'

'You mean,' said Zenda, 'as we say in French: *une machine extraordinaire!*'